Into the Fire

Death, Sex Slaves, and Drugs in South Vietnam

Death in the Dragon House House Book One

T. Martin O'Neil

PUBLICATION CONSULTANTS
PUBLISHING THE WORKS OF AUTHORS WORLDWIDE

PO Box 221974 Anchorage, Alaska 99522-1974
books@publicationconsultants.com—www.publicationconsultants.com

ISBN Number: 978-1-59433-693-5
eBook ISBN Number: 978-1-59433-694-2

Library of Congress Catalog Card Number: 2017930478

Manufactured in the United States of America.

Not in any way attempting to be trite, I dedicate *Into the Fire*, its characters, its message and its merits to the men and women of the Special Warfare community, regardless of branch of service. Without these men and women, much of the world we live in would not have the bright sunlight of peace. Most of the American public don't know what you really did, nor the sacrifices you've made. You do. To you may I sincerely say, Bravo Zulu – Well Done!

ACKNOWLEDGEMENTS

Once a person commits to the arduous life of Special Warfare, whether SEALS, Rangers, Special Air Groups (USAF), Commandos, Green Berets, Delta Force, Special Boat Teams, DEVGRU (SEAL Team 6), Force Recon (USMC), Inshore Undersea Warfare, or a number of classified groups and other assigned groups, it is a commitment for life. It doesn't go away with a piece of paper thanking that person for a job well-done and a flag in a shadow box. In fact, while there may be inter-service rivalries, every man and woman assigned to the care and keeping of special operations, is indeed special in their relationships to each other and to our nation, its Constitution and way of life. To them I am most grateful. Being part of this community reflects the highest order of admiration and support one can ever expect to give to his family, country, origins and even religion.

Another group often pushed from the limelight, but indeed should be the stars of the show, are the spouses and families of these operators. Without their timeless and unfailing support, special operators could never perform at the level they do.

Heading the above list of stars who is foremost in the limelight of my life, I thank my wife, Laurie, who has been my prime inspiration and support. Without her loving and tender understanding, I could never have opened this part of my memories with peace, knowing what I did was "better out than in." She and my children often had to endure the ravages of me recalling occurrences from the past even in my sleep. I say with the deepest brevity, I truly love you, your spouses and families.

What are we without heroes? The following men and women were my heroes and gave me their example, kindness and love thus permitting me to write about these times and memories.

At the top of this group are my father, mother and siblings. They've watched as I've endured the physical reconstruction of my body with kindness and love. They also endured the depth of my distance and solitude, even passion, at times affected by the events that from these injuries.

Standing close to the top of my hero list is *New York Times* Best Selling writer Marc Cameron who encouraged and pointed out my foibles as I endeavored to re-capture and write my thoughts. Thank you, most sincerely, Marc.

RADM Paul Speer (USN, ret), RADM G. Dennis Vaughan (USN, ret), the late RADM Bruce R. Boland (USN, ret), CAPT James D. Butler (USN, ret), CAPT Frank (Pappy) Schluntz (USN, ret), CAPT Eve J. Parrish (USN, ret), men and women of my six commands, and LtCol Darrell Zaugg (USAF) all encouraged me to write my experiences which helped significantly to remove the skeletons from my other side still darkly hanging with cobwebs in my mind. Each of these men and women are heroes to a person.

Definitely, not last nor least, is my publisher, Evan Swensen of Publications Consultants. I've had the good fortune of knowing him for more than a decade and in spite of that, he still liked me. He saw through my writing weaknesses and encouraged me to keep at it. Thank you, Evan.

FOREWORD

Into the Fire is the first of a three-novel series based on the life of Special Operations Intelligence Operator, Kevin S. Marks. Marks plies the struggle between honor, propriety, life and death against enemies of America and the American allies.

Mirroring the life of a real special forces operative, T. Martin O'Neil, the events cited are based on fact not fiction. Marty O'Neil is a 30-year plus veteran of the Naval Intelligence arena. Virtually all of his field time was spent with Special Warfare Units, and his insights into Southeast Asia are considerably different than what Hollywood or the press often portrayed. Names, and in some cases, locations have been modified, but the stories are based on actual events.

O'Neil demonstrates an intense need to keep the Free World vibrant and strong. His books bring to light uncomfortable secrets that were frequently swept under the rug due to so-called political correctness or hidden by politicians under the cloak of official secrecy. His story is the other side of the U.S. Navy's Special Warfare Teams—the human side.

O'Neil gives us a glimpse of quiet, secretive, subliminal ops. These operations didn't make the newspapers or the evening news. There is action, but not the way the movies often portray it—and it demonstrates why these men were called Special Operators. They were and are truly specially motivated.

The three books in the series, *Into the Fire, The Worth of Souls,* and *Not Their's to Take,* respectively reflect the missions and goals of counter-narcotics, counter-human trafficking, and counter-piracy. The first book reflects actions during the late years of the Vietnam War.

Enjoy it. I certainly did.

Marc Cameron
New York Times bestselling author of *Brute Force*

PROLOGUE: A REALITY CHECK

The first and second Vietnamese Wars

The U.S. involvement in the Second Vietnamese War was one of turmoil and frustration. The French had been in Southeast Asia since before World War II. In the first Vietnamese War, the French were driven out in 1954 after numerous protracted battles and losses in and around the village of Dien Bien Phu.

Dien Bien Phu was actually a series of battles that took place over almost four months. Viet Minh General Vo Nguyen Giap knew that forcing France to play a protracted and stall-oriented war would ultimately spell doom to the French support in Viet Nam and all of Southeast Asia. The French people drove their government into a peace accord using the tactic of a sympathetic liberal press.

Controlling the news media and politics at home was paramount in France's loss. Ultimately the United States would be led to abandonment of Southeast Asia using the same tactic. Giap's methods of terror, public relations and spin, are the key fighting elements of out-gunned, out-manned and less trained armies in virtually all modern wars of the last half of the twentieth as well as twenty-first centuries. Even regarding the events of radical Islamic terrorists, the liberal world turns a blind eye to what is really happening to actual victims due to so called political correctness.

Militarily, the French overpowered most Viet Minh (Vietnamese Communist) and Pathet Lao (Laotian Communist) advances. Likewise, the United States held the Viet Cong (Vietnamese Communist insurgents) and North Vietnamese Army at bey. Only when the ultra-liberal, media-driven popular support dried up from home, were the North Vietnamese and Viet Cong successful. To emphasize the point, Saigon and South Vietnam fell only a matter of months after the complete U.S. abandonment and military withdrawal in 1974.

The Domino Theory

The "Domino Theory" was frequently cited as a model which stated that if Vietnam fell to the Communists, then all of Southeast Asia would follow. Often this theory became the grounds for continuation of support and even escalation of the war.

Hindsight demonstrated the truth of the "Domino Theory." After Vietnam fell, Cambodia and to a large part Laos saw Communist aggression overcome their governments. Even Thailand's situation became tenuous at best. Thailand still today uses a balancing act with its multi-facet government which includes Communists and pro-Communists in crucial government positions thus controlling the affairs of state. Sometimes viewed as a bloodless revolution, the Communists controlling certain departments of the government permitted the country to be forced away from freedom and into bondage.

The Battles Late in the Second Vietnamese War

Just prior to the U.S. total military withdrawal in 1974, specifically from 1970-1973, much of the military support provided to South Vietnam was by Special Forces units from the Navy, Army, Marines, Air Force and Coast Guard. These small, seemingly insignificant battles fought and decisively won were normally omitted by the "objective" news media.

The activities of Special Forces Units, sometimes called generically Special Operations Groups (SOG) for ground-based units and SEALS for water-oriented units, covered many of the events of the "subliminal war" fought to help preserve freedom in Southeast Asia. Used interchangeably, these terms did not reflect the real nature of those who waged the combat and who were the successful combatants.

The Ho Chi Minh Trail

Throughout the Second Vietnamese War, movement of supplies and war materials from North Vietnam, Laos and Thailand and to some extent even Cambodia was accomplished using a manpower-intensive effort along what became known as the Ho Chi Minh Trail. In actuality, the trail was many parallel trails and even included the Mekong River. The Ho Chi Minh Trail used adjacent nations to attempt to secret arms and supplies into South Vietnam. The North Vietnamese Army and Viet Cong never observed national boundaries.

One tactic that was frequently successful in numerous areas was so-called carpet bombing. These attacks by the U.S. Air Force were often referred to as Arc Lights. They saturated areas using B-52 bombers dropping full loads of ordinance devastating huge paths of jungle and concentrations of both VC and NVA.

Special Forces units were also deployed to interdict these crucial supply lines. Thus many special operations sites were located close to trail branches sometimes only a few miles away.

The nature and story depicted in this book is set late in the U.S. involvement in that war. It is a book of fiction based on fact. Individual names were changed as well as many places to provide as much realism as can be expected from classified and inter-related declassified operations.

The Dragon

The lands of Southeast Asia, China and even Japan is resplendent with depictions of the dragon, its mystical powers and aggression. The people while not necessarily worshipping the dragon are most respectful of its powers. Like other societies and lands, fire of the dragon or serpent is depicted as all-consuming and all-powerful. It was a source of agonizing death. This power is only met and defeated by valiant warriors as well as special, mystical talismans and methods of combat.

Special Warfare Participants

This book and story is of a group of valiant warriors with marvelous powers. Such powers were frequently used and demonstrated by their uncanny abilities to out-think and out-fight their enemies casting fear into that enemy. Often these battles were a direct result of North Vietnamese atrocities and acts of terror. Again, those acts of terror were never mentioned by the liberal press. Undaunted, the Special Warfare operatives met the enemy and removed them with finality.

Bounties were paid by both the North Vietnamese and Viet Cong on Special Warfare operatives. Even today, special consideration is paid by their former enemies to those warriors who were part of the Special Warfare Groups in both Vietnamese Wars. Though greatly misguided, Hollywood depicts this group as wild and often ruthless, shunning authority and being anything but what real Special Warfare operatives were and are.

Unfortunate as it is, traitorous acts from within the South Vietnamese ranks and even from high-visibility American citizens caused many deaths to both American troops and their South Vietnamese counterparts. This was a tragic time and despite the well-meaning support of the U.S. military and sympathetic politicians, lack of support from the U.S. proper spelled the doom of a gentle, free and kind people.

Regardless of the politics, those that did serve honorably in the Second Vietnamese War brought the milk of human kindness to the people of South Vietnam, Thailand, Cambodia and Laos. Those who were antagonists brought fear and hopelessness to this land and people.

T. Martin O'Neil

CHAPTER I – NEW RULES

October, 1971 – Saigon, Republic of South Vietnam

Four days in South Vietnam and four rude awakenings. Lieutenant Junior Grade [LT(jg)] Kevin S. Marks could not believe how such an elite fighting force like the SEALs could be so effective and dedicated to their job yet have such horrible support. It seemed those holding the reigns making life and death decisions for them were as much against their success as the North Vietnamese or their Communist militia counterparts, the Viet Cong.

Marks was deep in thought. Already this was turning out to be a real discouraging first Monday with SEAL Team One, Detachment B. The eye-opening experience at Military Assistance Command, Vietnam (MACV), was certainly not what he'd expected.

First of all, MACV's Special Operations Group Intelligence Officer, Major Nelson Rodney LaRose, III, USAF, was nothing like Marks figured. LaRose was a tall man with fiery, red hair and matching disposition. He'd been assigned to work with Special Warfare Teams in Vietnam, but more specifically in the IV Corps area of operations which included the Mekong River Delta.

LCDR Randy Rogers, the Commanding Officer of SEAL Team One, Detachment B, accompanied Marks for his first foray into the house of the dragon that was to be MACV. He knew what to expect, but his knowledge didn't keep it from happening anyway.

Rogers was persona non gratis in LaRose's eyes, but the cool, calm, collected mannerisms of Marks only made matters worse as seen by

LaRose. It just confirmed that anyone associated with SEAL Team would be treated both rudely and crudely.

The drive back to An Tho, the compound location for the SEALS in IV Corps, was supposed to be in "safe" territory. "Safe" was a relative term in Vietnam. Both Marks and Rogers knew that a sniper or a rocket propelled grenade (RPG) from a hut or building along the way could ruin their day if they slowed down or let their minds wander.

Marks wondered if I Corps, II Corps or III Corps had relationships that were as difficult as they had with LaRose. He was sure that eventually this rude individual would meet his demise professionally whether from him or someone else.

Their stomachs rumbled as if on cue reminding them they had left too early for breakfast. If they continued back to the compound, they would miss lunch too, unless they stopped somewhere for something to eat. Stomachs won the battle.

Saigon had some great restaurants and great 'Mom and Pop gourmet' cuisine if you didn't mind monkey, dog, cat or rat. One learned never to ask what the meat was, just make sure it was well done. After all, it tasted just like chicken. The real 'code de cuisine' was eat, close your eyes and imagine it was steak and lobster. The good thing, however, were the spices. The smells created by the spices and combinations of ingredients were out of this world as well.

One small shop across from one of the many shopping bazaars had three outdoor tables with umbrellas. Umbrellas were a sure sign that the owner had enough money to feed well. It usually also meant that the restaurant had a large and regular clientele.

Bee pointed and motioned for Spoke to stop and pull over. Spoke parked their jeep, wedging it into a space behind a delivery truck and in front of a local cabby who stared sardonically at them. Spoke smiled apologetically at the cabby and waited for Bee to come around the Jeep. Together they walked over to one of the vacant tables and sat down.

The shopping bazaar across the street appeared to come right out of a tourist brochure. The scene was a montage of fragrances and colors.

Spices, open air butcher shops, human sweat, animals – mostly chickens and ducks, woks of hot cooking oil burning at the edges, oily exhaust from mopeds as well as cars and trucks, and a cacophony of noises all converged on the senses of people mingling on the street. Most had become oblivious to the combination, but Marks felt totally alive in that setting.

Talking, loud and agitated as well as softer and assured, entertained onlookers. Some haggling over the price of a piece of meat or bolt of cloth added to the noise and senses. Windows with thin cotton curtains moving with the faint, sultry breezes from second story rooms. Open French doors that exposed dark sometimes smoky interiors. Still, the most interesting were the colors, colors and more colors. These ranged from bright and intense to threadbare and faded.

Everything grabbed the eyes, noses and ears baptizing on-lookers with an air of total immersion into the Vietnamese culture. It was a gift of sensory delight, indeed a colorful feast.

LCDR Rogers, like most members of elite teams, and that included aviators, had a nickname. Most nicknames were inside jokes among fellow team members. His was Bee – short for Beeman, a potent clove-flavored gum he always seemed to be chewing.

Marks also had a handle that reflected his first duty assignment at Commander in Chief, Pacific Fleet (CINCPACFLT). His nickname came from an experience in the front office while there. His four-year-old son accompanied him one day to the office. While visiting the front office, the Admiral wanted to get to know this young recruit and so asked him what his father did for the Navy. Without hesitation, he said his dad was a "spoke." Meaning a spook, the nickname stuck and Marks' handle remained Spoke.

Now, here he was in Saigon, South Vietnam, being immersed completely into the Vietnamese experience. Jarring him from his inner thoughts was a beautiful young waitress.

The smiling girl wore a simple, traditional, dark-blue, wrap-around Vietnamese Ao Dai dress with a choker neck line and short sleeves. She came up to the table and offered an English menu along with forks, spoons and napkins. Bee shook his head to the eating utensils, but accepted the napkin and menu. He imitated the eating style of chop sticks and the little girl giggled. She was beautiful and had a smile that would have melted any hardcore GI.

She turned to Spoke with the same offer. He too refused the eating utensils but accepted the napkin and menu. She gave him a smile and a giggle too. Spoke knew he was going to appreciate being here in South Vietnam if for nothing else but the kids. His three at home flashed in his mind and he wanted to see them again even for just a moment.

"What's good?" Spoke asked Bee.

"Just look at somebody's plate and point. It's all good," was the reply. "Don't worry about the meat. It all tastes like chicken. Just make sure it's well done." Bee smiled at his own humor.

Their waitress giggled again and between the pointing and charades that followed took their order. The enterprising, giggling young waitress quickly ran into the back and passed along the request. In less than three minutes, a steaming bowl of rice and soup arrived at the table. Spoke thought it smelled heavenly. His stomach was rumbling, reminding him of the long day and lack of sustenance. He was famished.

The little girl went back to the kitchen and came out still smiling. After hesitating and looking both ways at the street curb, she scurried over to the bazaar to pick up some items to help her mother and sister in the kitchen. Turning to smile and wave at the two officers, she headed into the first shop.

The concussion of the explosion was deafening, splitting the air with noise, smoke, fire and debris. One moment the happiness of a young girl's smile, the next the gut-wrenching realization of a scene of mangled bodies, hardware, fires and smoke. The smell of burning flesh, burning stalls and people running everywhere was mind-numbing. How could this happen? How could such a gentle and civilized people do this to each other?

Bee and Spoke opened the flaps of their holsters, grabbed their Colt .45 Automatic handguns and raced for their jeep.

Judging from the debris and fire, this was more than just a satchel charge. The Viet Cong had been experimenting with enhanced explosive devices and may have used a vehicle loaded with additional explosives or propane bottles. From the apparent damage, a timer attached to a satchel charge was probably the initiating device. Their jeep had been saved from the effects of the blast by the delivery van parked in front of them.

The little girl's mother ran into the street screaming her name, pleading with all that would listen that her daughter was in that inferno.

Spoke felt sick. The kind of sick that forced the foul taste of bitter bile into his throat. Not just nausea, but sick all the way to his soul. He knew it was pedal to the metal. For all, he knew the two officers were the intended targets. They didn't want any more collateral damage. In their eyes, the deck was stacked against them and they would choose another day to demonstrate heroism.

Unfortunately, the thoughts of that little girl would always haunt both men in their thoughts and nightmares.

The drive back was quiet and emotionally draining. Both wanted to attack anyone and anything that might be part of this travesty. Spoke's thoughts were of his children. What if that had happened to his family? What would he do? What could he do? His inner-most response said to protect his family by standing and facing his enemy. His reality was that he couldn't even point or identify the enemy. He couldn't face them. His only emotional reflex left no winners, only losers.

CHAPTER 2 – THE BETRAYAL

It was a long night for Spoke. Thoughts of the attack haunted his dreams. He did not sleep well. That alone was bad enough, but going to work the next day meant he had to get his head in the game.

The first operation was supposed to be a "safe" operation. Spoke knew being a "safe op" meant there was at least a target folder with maybe some pictures. Who knew how old the pictures were or even whether the target still existed since the folder was at least a year old, maybe more.

Bee joined him. The two officers carefully poured over the target folder but more importantly the photos in the target folder. These photos were obviously provided by an Air Force RF-4. Reconnaissance missions were not the primary role of the air superiority fighter. Therefore, reconnaissance missions by F-4 aircraft sometimes left a bit to be desired. The pilot's rapid movements or jinking meant there was probably good reason. No doubt enemy small arms fire.

Since the photos were almost a year old much of the fine detail may have changed. However, the aircraft movement did little to help the quality of the photos.

Both men knew reconnaissance missions were extremely dangerous and required a special kind of pilot as well as specialized equipment. The early RF-4 planes were air-superiority aircraft and used a pod under the wing, filled with cameras and other sensors modified for this role. While useful, it wasn't quite like the quality of the RA-5C Vigilante aircraft of the Navy.

The selected point of ingress for this operation was a helicopter landing zone (HLZ) blasted out of the jungle some 13 months before by a BLU-82 commonly known as a 'Daisy Cutter' – a huge 12,600-lb metal container with a parachute on one end to keep it oriented correctly and a long, lance-like 20-foot spike opposite the parachute on the other. The BLU-82 was a large pressurized cylinder which contained ammonium nitrate and aluminum powder in a GSX slurry. On impact, it would rupture forcing the pressurized mixture into the surrounding jungle trees and plant-life. Then, delayed igniters caused the mixture to explode. The resulting explosion destroyed enough area to permit helicopters to land. The best part was the lack of crater. It cut and destroyed the trees and plant life as well as any small huts or buildings, but left the area easily usable for troop maneuvering. The radius varied but some could be as large as 150-meters.

Since this was over a year later, the condition today might be iffy at best. As fast as the jungle recaptured itself, it was a crap shoot as to whether the HLZ could even be recognized. The bright spot was that at least there was information and pictures this time. Fortunately, satellite imagery confirmed that there did exist a break in the trees at that location. Was it adequate to use as an HLZ? Local "eyes on the ground" said it was.

The HLZ was about two and a half miles west of the target. Rendezvous with the Army of the Republic of Vietnam (ARVN) Special Operations soldiers was to be at 0230.

The op was a simple "snatch" of a new village chieftain recently put in place by the Viet Cong. Seems the previous chief was pro-US and had reportedly suffered from an extremely bad skin condition. He had to have it all peeled off while he was still alive, staked out and in front of his wife and family as well as the whole village. Amazing how that story was never mentioned by the Peacenicks or Washington Post, thought Marks.

This "safe op" was to snatch the newly placed chief ("the package") and be back to the HLZ by 0400 for extraction. Easy, right? Whoever thought of these names must be some idiot, thought Spoke, safely hidden away from any action in a basement with no windows and no contact with intelligent life. No "op" was "safe" much less a package delivery service.

Rogers, also, kept trying to convince himself that this was a simple op. "The only easy day was yesterday" read the sign above the door right below the large "Return with Honor" sign. He'd heard these two phrases since BUDS – Basic Underwater Demolition School. It was ingrained into every SEAL.

The equipment pre-check showed the various shades of green glow emanating from the night observation devices (NODS), enlarged telescope-like devices that amplified the existing light and provided the user the ability to see in the subdued light of night. Their chief problem was battery-life and ruggedness. While usable, the alternative to the NODS was total blackness. This operation would take advantage of no moon. It would have already set when they departed. Deep in the jungle, the starlight would not provide much ambient light either.

Gathering the team, Bee led them to the helo pad. There, two Army UH-1 Hueys were preparing to lift off. Once on board, the team buckled in and each man gave the thumbs up sign for "ready to go." Bee signaled the pilot. Each chopper then lifted off with its cargo of SEALS.

Eighteen minutes later, the two Hueys touched down. The elephant grass was already over 4 feet high. The helos flattened the grass permitting a circular landing site. So far so good.

Roger's men jumped out and headed for predetermined locations around the HLZ perimeter and then just as quickly the Hueys were off again. Once in position, men would raise their arms signifying they were safe and ready. In the dark, the telescope-like NODS would permit Rogers to know where each member of the team was. Minutes ticked by. Strict radio silence was observed.

The distant whop-whop-whop of two additional Hueys broke the intense, dark silence. The unmistakable sounds of the helos increased in intensity. Mimicking the U.S. SEALS, the ARVN Special Ops soldiers exited their aircraft. Just as quickly, the Hueys lifted off.

The teams were to remain stationary until the helos departed and sounds returned to a semblance of normal. The grass and other foliage whipped around. Smells of aviation fuel exhaust, cut grass and decaying vegetation filled noses.

What an odd combination thought Rogers. It would have been an interesting smell in another part of the world and another time.

All remained as quiet as a morgue. Two minutes dragged by. Night jungle sounds rapidly returned to normal.

"Raven One this is Tiger One, over," the ARVN Team leader quietly whispered. His microphone was a throat mike, a microphone tightly held against his throat by an elastic band. His accented voice was steady but clearly sounded concerned. His heavy Vietnamese accent made communications a challenge never-mind having to speak English through a throat mike.

It was a good thing Rogers' team had trained these men. Communications, and communications discipline, would be much more effective than when they first met six months before. They had been on other ops together and it appeared the training was paying off.

"Roger, Tiger One, move your men one hundred meters east to the edge of the LZ."

Since they were all together, the ARVN leader raised his hand and motioned to his team. His men spread out in a tight pattern and moved together. Some of the best training in the world was clearly being demonstrated here.

The teams quietly linked up. Soft greetings out of the way, they all gathered and started toward the target. Most of the U.S. SEALS knew their ARVN counterparts as they had grown close during their training and previous action. They were brothers in arms. They had bonded. It didn't matter what color their skin or their language, they'd been tried in the crucible of battle and been forged as one.

Following their leaders, the men of both units moved together like a well-rehearsed dance team. Overlap of each gap was filled virtually without looking. Each man sensed and knew where his counterpart was. Rapidly the men moved through the jungle toward their goal.

Half an hour later, the unmistakable sound of the RPG rocket motor was the first indication of something very, very wrong. They were only about a mile from the target village. Everyone went face down and tried to fan out so as not to be flanked. Training immediately kicked in. Pairs of men on the outside of the formation went back to back so as to have a full 360-degree clear field of fire. Each man strained to see into the undergrowth.

Almost simultaneously, all hell broke loose. Three mortar shells exploded in the middle of the group – probably captured US M-2 mortars or Type 31 60mm Chinese Communist copies of the M-2. The unmistakable sound of AK-47's followed by the faster and higher pitched M-16's as well as other arms filled the night.

The M-16's, M-14's, M-2 carbines, shotguns and M-60 machine guns turned the previously quiet jungle into a bedlam of deadly light and noise. Green tracers were the bad guys. Red tracers were good. Each man tried to follow the confluence of the green tracers to their origin, and the bad guy attached to them.

The acrid smell of burning powder and the deafening rifle fire seemed amplified because of the proximity to the trees and overhead canopy of limbs and leaves. Explosions as well as screams of pain filled the darkness. Those men who had the NODS tried looking away from their night vision devices fearing the flashes of explosions and gunfire would blind them.

Two more mortar shells exploded almost in the same location as the first three. It was obvious that these mortars had been previously "sighted in." It was an ambush, plain and simple. At first blush, it appeared someone had sent the teams in to be slaughtered – indeed a traitor.

Another mortar shell blew up beside the ARVN SOF Commander sending his body flying like a rag doll being thrown from a speeding car.

The scream of "Medic! Medic!" filled the night even above the sound of exploding grenades and rifle fire. Enemy and friendly fire concentrated on every flash point observed. Flash hiders on rifles seemed like they were useless. The concussive over-pressure of the explosions deafened everyone in the area.

Where were they?! Bad guys seemed to be everywhere! Rogers daisy-chained commands to his closest team members so they could pass on directives. They were in a loose crescent-shaped position now, but needed to move out to counter a flanking maneuver by the enemy. This also allowed the SEALS to hopefully get around the opposition positions.

Then, as quickly as it started, the firing stopped. Ears continued to ring. Eyes and noses were smarting from the burning powder and flashes of light. Some of the men who had NODS had the presence of mind to get them operational again, but most just tried to make sense of the past minute.

Even experienced warriors took a second to try to make sense of what just happened. Extensive training helped at such a time, but until one experienced it, training can only go just so far. The entire elapsed time had been right at a minute, maybe even less. Who's keeping time when your head is on the line and in the dirt?

"Raven 2, Raven 1. Sitrep," Rogers urgently whispered into his throat mike.

"Raven 1, Raven 2. Two wounded, minor and ambulatory," came back the reply.

"Tiger 1, Raven 1. Sitrep," Rogers again whispered into his mike.

Everything was quiet.

"Tiger 1, this is Raven 1. Sitrep!" The plea from Rogers sounded in his voice even though he willed it to be professional. Major Phoc Do Che had been a personal friend and he prayed it was only a communication glitch. This better not be bad news, he thought.

"Raven 1, Tiger 2. Not good. Tiger 1 KIA and three badly wounded," was the reply.

Rogers fumed with frustration and anger. This had to be an ambush set up by some loose-lipped traitor either at MACV or within the ARVN ranks. This was not going to happen on his watch. Rogers was going to find out. And heaven help the SOB that did this.

The exfiltration, or exfil, became much more difficult since timeline, verification, and extraction had been hampered with the urgency and medevac needs of the teams. Concern for safety in returning to their point of insertion was paramount. Bee did not want a continuation of the slaughter the teams had just experienced only a few minutes before.

It took them almost two hours as they covered their retreat to the HLZ. Without the wounded and dead, it previously took them only a half hour. They would not leave anyone behind and so it took much longer to cover the same distance.

CHAPTER 3 - ACCOUNTABILITY

0830, Monday, 1 November 1971 – Military Assistance Command, Vietnam Headquarters, Saigon

The two young U.S. Naval officers entered the large double doors and moved down the corridor. The glass in the doors was semi-opaque, darkish green but see-through, signifying bullet and explosive resistant. Having already passed through security at the gate, they were free to pass wherever they needed inside the massive building except in areas that had "island security." Island security usually manifest itself as heavy glass windows and additional security personnel at the door.

Turning right, and down three doors, they entered a very non-descript office with another heavy, bullet-resistant glass window and pass-through slot at the bottom of the window. Sort of reminded LCDR Rogers of the no-tell motels he'd seen and that brought a smile to his face. The smells of stale cigarette, cigar and pipe tobacco as well as the hint of stale booze assaulted the nose. Someday, thought Rogers, the military would ban smoking from its offices.

The young Army Corporal behind the glass greeted the officers and asked for their identification. The Corporal knew one of the officers very well, but the formality was imposed due to their proximity to the General's office within.

"Good to see you Commander. Just a moment," he said and turned away. LDCR Rogers and Lt(jg) Marks, waited to be buzzed in. MACV HQ Intelligence Office had been nicknamed "Inner Sanctum" due to the bizarre and seemingly stupid things that emanated from this particular building and office.

"Please come in gentlemen. The Major is expecting you." The buzzer on the door lock was loud and very noticeable.

"I'll bet he is," mumbled Bee with an obvious tone of animosity not directed at the Corporal, but at the frustration this office and that major forced into his mind.

Behind two sets of cubicles loomed a large vault door. Both men passed into the vault and turned left. Standing there waiting was the tall LaRose. His attitude matched his fiery red hair. He hated SEAL Team and referred to them as the sniveling brats of the SPECWAR world. He tried every week to give SEALS the dirtiest and least attractive assignments possible. His personal goal was to see them fail and make fools of them. His was a war of seething, inner hate from long ago. Rumor had it that a SEAL had taken the love of his life and left him with a very deep, emotional laceration and resulting scar.

"Here's your list of *prioritized* assignments. I'm sure you will find them to your liking. They're easy enough." His icy directive in tone and content implied his personal hatred. He hesitated to wait for the impending retort he knew would come from Rogers.

Quickly trying to save face and get the first shots in, he flatly stated to Spoke, "Well, Lieutenant, are they treating you like dirt?"

"Thank you, no, Sir," responded Marks neutrally.

"If you know what's good for you, Lieutenant, keep these men focused on their work," added LaRose in his usual condescending manner. The reference to the more senior rank of Naval "Lieutenant" was customary when addressing either a LT(jg) or Lieutenant. "Commander" for a Lieutenant Commander or Commander. Normally such references only occurred in a more casual environment and not in official communications.

In this case, Spoke swung at the opening pitch and Bee later would say to the rest of the team, hit a home run. 'Saving face' was not in Spoke's lexicon even though he had been in-country for just over a week. Instead of acquiescing to the pressure of the moment, he turned the tables on the Major and forced him into an embarrassing and extremely defensive position.

"Sir, of those assigned ops, may we see the target folders?" he asked almost absentmindedly. No one had apparently ever requested the necessary background for any ops before, just assuming they would be given all the necessary materials. With this seemingly innocent question, Spoke made sure life would never be the same from "Inner Sanctum" or from "Big Red," the new nickname he'd decided to give LaRose.

It caught the Major completely off guard. He was too stunned to reply with any kind of smart remark. The question was seemingly innocent and yet told of a level of experience far beyond his apparent pay grade. It also demonstrated that he'd had experience dealing with superiors far above Big Red's pay grade as well.

"Just a minute," LaRose muttered and turned to the Air Force Tech Sergeant standing by. He motioned for him to get the requested items. Then turning away, the Major moved over to his desk and away from the two naval officers.

Five minutes later, the TSgt returned and reported there were only five of the 17 ops with folders. Spoke looked at the folders and turned back to Bee.

"I guess that makes it a real easy week, Skipper. Of the five we have folders for, only three are within our operational mandates."

SEALS were given specific duties and reported directly to the Commander in Chief, Pacific Fleet, through the fleet commander, Seventh Fleet. They were simply there to augment the needs from MACV on an "as needed" basis, not to be the prime movers for the Army Green Berets, Rangers or Marine Recon teams. Unfortunately, individuals like Major LaRose, who saw it as their mission in life to discredit the SEALS, refused to even try to understand this role or mission.

Bee turned to Big Red and smugly said, "We'll see you next week and thanks for the light week. Please let us help you any way we can. Oh, and the CINCPACFLT Rep wanted us to remind you that we don't work as your 'on call' whipping boys. Don't make it a habit of pulling the crap you pulled last week. It only demonstrates your ineptitude."

Big Red, already primed and ready for Bee's broadside, screamed "You prima donna bastards. You'll damned well do what I assign or I'll have your command for willful disobedience!" The quiet in the office outside of the vault was deafening. Everyone from the Intelligence Office to the General's Office heard him.

"You can try, but it won't happen here or in this lifetime," responded Bee lightly and as cool as a cucumber. "Oh, and another thing, if I find out who sold us out on that 'snatch' op last week, I'll make sure he sings soprano forever."

Both Naval officers turned and walked out. At the front door, the Corporal smiled and motioned a stealthy thumbs-up.

"CORPORAL!" came a scream from an extremely agitated voice out of sight.

Ah well, thought Spoke, the price of working and dealing with the shallow end of the gene pool. He also wondered what the General thought of such unprofessionalism. Surely there had to be accountability.

CHAPTER 4 – MORE FLACK

Early the next morning after the visit to MACV in Saigon and after the so-called "safe op," Bee was still too pumped up with adrenaline to sleep. He knew he needed sleep, but he was way too angry to do anything but fume. Even cleaning his weapons had not helped reduce his anger. He went to his makeshift office in the SEAL Team compound.

The phone bag rang next to Bee's small combat desk. He answered it on the second ring and immediately a pall came over his face and entire demeanor. He obviously knew the caller by voice. More than that, it was obvious he resented that person even more. The response was terse and to the point.

"Look, *Major*, we are not modifying our workload without prior authorization from CINCPACFLT...... I don't care what *you* feel is important. You had the chance yesterday to give us the op along with the necessary support information *and* a target folder...... I can't help it if you choose to pull your slimy tricks on us. Get your Ranger buddies to do their job for a change instead of sending us out on wild goose chases because they couldn't hack it....... Well you take it up with CINCPACFLT's rep there in Saigon. If he feels it is in our operational responsibility, and you have the proper intelligence this time, I'll be in there on Monday..... And don't worry, I'll also be calling him!" Bee slammed the phone receiver into the canvas bag.

"Damn that jerk!" Bee said turning to the Senior Chief Petty Officer who doubled as both the Administration Officer and one of the best gunners on the team.

"Now all of a sudden he wants us to cover for his precious Rangers who've obviously screwed up an op in III Corps. I don't mind doing it the right way, but sending us in with no intel and no pictures, just so he can get his fair-haired boys another Army gedunk ribbon is beyond right or fair."

A gedunk ribbon was what many military personnel, regardless of branch, called a ribbon or medal that was just given out, regardless of whether it was earned or deserved, and basically just decorated the wearer's chest – chest candy or fruit salad to the uninitiated.

"I'm really close to taking him out behind the wood shed," Bee almost screamed. He continued fuming for several minutes.

The Senior Chief nodded. He'd heard this rant before. Attempting to change the subject and lighten up the mood, he politely said, "Sir, we got range scores from this morning's qualifications. Seems our new Intel Officer is a pretty good shot – 298 out of 300 with the .45 and smoked everyone else on the Sphincter Course."

The Sphincter Course was the nickname for a heavily pressured tactical course that had everything except someone shooting back. Your own worst enemy was between your ears.

Still fuming over Big Red's call, Bee tersely responded, "Yeah, but let's get someone shooting back at him and then see how he does. Get him in here as soon as he gets back from weapons cleaning."

Everyone pitched in and cleaned weapons after any kind of shoot or op. Their weapons were their lifeblood and had to always be in the very best meticulous condition possible.

"Aye, Sir," responded the Senior Chief.

Returning to the range area, the Senior Chief spotted Spoke and walked over to him.

"Hey Spoke. Skipper wants to see you."

Marks turned away from the ammo boxes and acknowledged the Senior Chief. "Thanks, Senior. Any clue what it's about?"

"Not really, but I think it might be something about that MAJ LaRose over at MACV."

Spoke thought out loud, "Great, how can Big Red screw up our day today?"

Finishing cleaning, Spoke headed over to the CO's office.

Entering, he smiled and noted immediately Bee's demeanor. This was not the time for a quirky joke or cute comment.

"How's the planning for the ammo/POL (petroleum, oil and lubricants) dump 'demolition' op?" Bee's question was flat-lined. "If it's not done by noon, and in my hand, we'll have wasted a perfectly good day."

"Yes, Sir. It's not only done, but ready for your review," Spoke responded evenly and not confrontational in any way. "I finished it before the guys invited me to go qualify at the range this morning. Since you were indisposed at the time, I went with them."

"Look, Lieutenant, I know you can shoot. I saw your jacket from CINCPACFLT."

The 'jacket' followed every person to every new command and was a basic personnel file.

"You can probably outshoot almost everyone on the team from the shooting line, but out there, real people are shooting back and trying to kill you and your team members. Let's keep focused on the work here."

"Yes, Sir. When would you like to review the plan?"

Spoke again responded not in the frustrated manner he'd been addressed, but in the professional manner he'd done with his father, grandfather and every other commanding officer he'd had. He knew the frustration of command and the pressures not only of lives on the line but of all the variables that made the Commanding Officer's role the difficult dichotomy it was. On one side, the leadership fun of the Team, but on the other side the knowledge that if you screwed up, you had to face the families, commanders and horrors of knowing their deaths were all on you.

"Assemble the team and be in the Ready Room in 30 minutes."

"Aye, Skipper."

"And there's an extra dessert as well as a gold star for your forehead if you include getting rid of that damned LaRose," Bee added the comment as his frustrated way of trying to lighten the mood.

CHAPTER 5 – THE NEW GUY'S PLAN

Rogers stood before the 16 assembled men. "Gentlemen, this ammo dump and POL storage area is our target. You will note its relationship to Saigon. We believe it is where Charlie (military slang for bad guys to US personnel in Southeast Asia) is getting all his explosives and ammo for the attacks inside Saigon like the one Spoke and I were in last week. I have personally reviewed the attack plan from Lieutenant (jg) Marks. It is solid and provides both excellent ingress and egress procedures. Please note we will be in a divided attack. I'm sure I don't need to caution you about making sure of your target. No friendly fire incidents on my watch. Spoke will now brief you on the details of the terrain, ingress and egress."

Marks began pointing at the map on the tripod easel, "Gentlemen, the two teams will leave via riverine boats at 2330. For Charlie's benefit, we will appear to be moving away from the dump and rendezvous at point Alpha with our assigned Swift Boat Squadron. Both teams will split up using two boats each and move to point Bravo and Charlie respectively. You will note that each ingress point is on opposite sides of the dump. Team One will then move to point Delta near the west side of the objective. Allowing one hour for any cross-country SNAFUs, Team Two will simultaneously move to point Echo. At about 0330, and confirmed by a quick burst radio transmission, Team One will launch its attack against the guards and billeting huts. Allowing one minute for response from sleepy guards and sleeping men to establish a full defensive posture against the attack, Team Two will launch its strike against the ammo and POL from the opposite side.

"It is critical that Charlie's response forces have initial time to turn their backs to the ammo. This will create a focused response against Team One and reduce support from behind their position. From most recent photos and human intelligence (HUMINT), the ammo is the most-heavily guarded part of the site. POL will generate the biggest show initially and should get them to lower their guard on the ammo. HUMINT also indicates that the entire dump is guarded by VC (Viet Cong militia) not NVA (North Vietnam Army) regulars. This is to our advantage for the confusion factor. Don't underestimate the VC, but experience has demonstrated that since Tet, they are not the seasoned fighters they used to be. They also confuse easily. Their command and control is far less than the North Vietnamese regulars."

Everyone there knew that since the Tet offensives of 1968 and 1970, the NVA and Viet Cong had been severely hurt with numbers of experienced soldiers. While they were inexperienced, they were learning rapidly about being under fire.

"Egress is at point Foxtrot for both teams. Charlie will most likely think we will head for the closest extraction point. You will note that Foxtrot is overland and away from our normal wet extraction. Swift Boats will pick us up at this point.

"Alternate extraction is point Xray. This is west of a village north of the dump. Extraction there will be via helo, but is tenuous at best. The village has been friendly in the past, but may be in question at the present time. This is why Foxtrot is our best choice.

"I have an annotated map for each team leader."

Bee stepped forward. "Any questions?"

Hearing none, he indicated that he would lead Team Two and the XO, Lieutenant Johann Swolchowski, affectionately called 'Swede,' would lead Team One. He then split up the team so that each group had the necessary help to fulfill its part of the op.

"Spoke, a word," Bee's tone was subdued and almost confidential.

"Yes, Sir."

Pulling him aside, Bee began, "Look.... earlier...."

"Skipper, please. I come from a long line of commanding officers. I know and will do the best job I can to make this team not only successful but honorable too." Marks looked up at the Return with Honor sign over the door.

Bee looked down. "Thanks and keep thinking outside the box. Some of these guys are still so new that they haven't been exposed to different or complex attack strategies. This is their introduction."

The SEAL armory was a large, heavily secured CONEX (steel shipping container) in an earthen revetment that would permit the container to blow up rather than out in the event of an accidental explosion or the result of an enemy shell. There, each man on the op received the necessary explosives and ammo to do his job. They checked their buddy for anything astray and that their face paint was in place. Then they turned to someone else to make sure they'd not missed anything, either. Quietly, in muffled tones, they confirmed each had the correct load-out. Spoke watched and felt the anxiety of a mother sending her kids off for their first day of Kindergarten. He'd only been with the team for going on two weeks but already had strong emotional ties to each. This was *his* plan, and he felt the weight of responsibility on his shoulders.

Bee walked over to him. "Want to go?"

"In a heartbeat," came Spoke's quick reply.

"Give it time. Let's see how everyone responds to the new guy's plans. You know the rules and the regulations regarding Intel Officers and combat, but maybe in the future we'll see about letting you in on the workload. The regs say nothing about HUMINT missions anyway."

Spoke had been trained in HUMINT and here was his ticket to the dance.

Spoke almost stopped breathing. *What did he say?!*

CHAPTER 6 – THE PLAN'S OUTCOME

The afternoon drug on. Dinner-time passed. The team left on time to link with their Riverine Squadron partners. After cleaning his eating utensils, Spoke walked over to the radio shack and leaned inside. Red lights made for a subdued appearance inside. Small lights blinked and flashed.

The smell of stale, burnt coffee and stale cigarettes assaulted his nose in the closed-in confines of the radio shack. While he was in there, Spoke had ordered all smoking be outside. It was dark and he knew just how irritating it had been to walk into a wall of smoke from someone's lit, concealed smoke. While he felt if they wanted to ruin their own lungs, fine, just don't ruin his.

He'd adopted the irritated and frustrated manner he'd seen Bee take last night. He knew it was wrong, but he really felt the frustration and it made him short-tempered.

Spoke paced back and forth. He needed to know. Had his plan worked? Casualty count. What was going on? He hated the radio silence. "Any word yet?"

"No, Sir. Not since you asked three minutes ago."

This was the frustration, the angst, of waiting.

Five minutes passed. Then ten. What was going on? They should have been back in contact. No distress calls had gone out for Xray. Did that mean they were alright, or that they were still engaged? Was it always like this?

Without asking, RM2 Robert Stewart commented, "Welcome to my world. Until it's in the can, you never know. It's like sending out the kids to the store and then waiting to hear back that they're alright. It's hell. This whole thing is maddening as hell."

Five more minutes passed. Spoke continued to pace back and forth.

"It only *seems* like it helps but truthfully it only wears out boots or the floor, Sir," the RM2 quietly commented.

Spoke looked again at the clock for the hundredth time. 0453. Had the clock stopped?

Suddenly a short transmission filled the room with statically charged noise. "Recovery complete. Returning to base." Spoke almost wanted to scream and dance. That wouldn't do for proper decorum, but who gave a damn. He still didn't have all the answers yet, but they were alive and at least no casualty reports severe enough to require Medevac. His mind spoke the unspeakable, thank heaven above.

Eight minutes later, a further report. "All members accounted for. No casualties. Target destroyed. Snake Charmer, out." Snake Charmer was the code name assigned to the team prosecuting this action. The Operation was part of Mongoose, a multi-service, multi-national move to eradicate the arms build-up in the Mekong Delta at the end of the Ho Chi Minh Trail.

The team arrived back at the compound by 0630. Now came the very tired and hopefully short debrief of the operation.

Bee stood in front of 46 very tired, very hungry, very emotionally charged men. The riverine and swift boat crews were also there. "Gentlemen, we succeeded. This will set Charlie back months, even years. Execution was excellent. Next time, Senior Chief, how about using a bit more C4 to start things off. We are not being rationed." Snickers from the assembled men. "The response time was outstanding and could not have been better if we had directed and choreographed their response ourselves. The only real sticky part was the new guard tower. We did not know they would have a 12.7 weapon there. Fortunately, the plan was to take out the tower early and that negated the use of it." The 12.7mm heavy machine gun was the Soviet answer to the .50-cal M2 of the US.

"It would also be appropriate to check the batteries on the NODS. Two of them crapped out. We can't take chances out there, especially on longer operations."

Turning to the boat operators he continued, "Extraction could improve. When we split our team, we have to take into consideration that your Fast Boats may be used to support Army pukes. They need a bit more primping time to get into position." Again, more snickers. "You did the right thing in setting a perimeter at the extraction point. Something we need to plan for in the future." He looked over at Spoke.

Spoke thought to himself, mental note: plan for extraction point perimeter for the next op.

"Incidentally, Spoke, great plan." Several men gave it a half-hearted applause. "Now go and get your weapons cleaned, get some chow and let's get some shuteye. Spoke, a minute." After the public, vocal praise, Spoke thought, now how did I screw up?

"We have a recon op of another village for MACV. This one is off the books, but I need a set of eyes that understands what makes that village so important. Know anybody that could help?"

Spoke almost burst out loud. "I'll check around and let you know in about a second…. Yes, seems I found a volunteer."

"Get me a plan for this sector and this village." Bee pointed to a small intersection of roads northwest of Saigon. "Remember, this is a clandestine **recon** only. Happy snaps and village layout. Get it to me by 1800."

The only important thing Spoke could even think of in that area was the Army's helo base at Tay Ninh. There were two converging Mekong River tributaries and triple canopy vegetation, but why was this location so hot? Why Rangers couldn't do this was anyone's guess, but it didn't surprise him that Bee would have been so angry at Big Red for trying to use SEALs to do Army's job. After all, the Army boys had probably partied too hardy and needed their beauty sleep.

He'd never harbored much dislike for any of the Special Forces Units until coming in-country and watched who did the heavy lifting and who got the credit. He was positive that farther north in I and II Corps, Army was doing its job just fine, but up there they had Marine Recon to do their heavy lifting. No doubt the Army boys would get the credit and probably a gedunk ribbon for SEAL Team's trouble. Seemed like Army always had a ribbon, patch, or award for virtually everything they did, not that awards were why he and others did their job, but for once, he'd hoped credit would be given where credit was due. This wasn't Cub Scouts any more. It was life and death, not a game.

Spoke looked at the map. Since there were no available pictures, the only thing he could imagine was to look at mission histories and possibly maps.

A topographic or topo map didn't yield much either. The terrain was virtually flat. No wonder Big Red wanted someone else to peek under the walls of the tent - then send in his "wonder boys" to get the credit. He was already sounding like the rest of the team as far as the Army Rangers were concerned.

Alright. He'd do what he could to show neutrality and perhaps mend fences and to hell with Big Red. He reached for the telephone. He called the CINCPACFLT rep in Saigon on the secure line. The secure line was an encrypted phone that scrambled the signal. A similar receiver on the other end would unscramble the transmission and make it legible.

There had to be someone that had been in that village before. Maybe they even knew what was so important about it. Hopefully, someone there could help. Obviously since Big Red had alienated himself from every major command in MACV, Spoke had to get the information himself.

Fifteen minutes later, he had what little could be gleaned from the CINCPACFLT rep's office. Seems a Marine Recon unit had traveled north to interdict a branch of the Ho Chi Minh Trail a year ago in III Corps. They'd been through the area and had some pictures as well as descriptions. There was a messenger leaving for Bien Hoa in about an hour. If that messenger could bring whatever info the Marines had to An Tho, he could be there by 1600 or so. Naturally, unless 'Murphy' raised his ugly head, he'd have the info needed to perform his job.

Without any real info about the area, the only thing he could do now was wait. He thought also about what he needed to take to "observe" this target. He would need his camera, his 1911 Colt .45ACP, preferably his suppressed MAC-10 also in .45ACP, his Fairbairn-Sykes stiletto and a mindset that would help him get through this night. He wasn't even a little sleepy. He was going to the ball! What could he wear?!

CHAPTER 7 – THINKING OUTSIDE THE BOX

Bee looked carefully at the drawings of the village Spoke had drawn. Tay Ninh would be the closest drop-in point. Because the operation was in Cambodia, this would have to be a very delicate matter. Covert ops at its best. Spoke called it right, again.

A disinformation radio stream pinpointing Xa Vo Dat to the northeast as the target ingress point would be an ideal diversion. If there were any NVA or even VC troops in the area, hopefully they would be lulled into a false sense of security. Doubtful, but one could always hope.

Next, Bee looked at the area on the maps Spoke had obtained. The questions came quickly, "How did you get these? Why weren't they at MACV?" Then realizing the answer to his own question, he continued, "That damned LaRose is so stinking lazy. He can't even figure out what holdings he has or has access to. Instead he sends us to do his dirty work so he can claim that he is the 'all-powerful.' Hopefully, you figured out how we can give him a ride down memory lane."

"Not this time, Skipper, but don't give that extra dessert away too soon. He may have done this to himself this time. I'll fill you in after we're done." Spoke had a plan thanks to the CINCPACFLT rep. Big Red was playing into it nicely.

Spoke then outlined the operational plan which was for a small group, four or five men at most. Those details would be left to Bee as the commander. That would be critical. The number had to be small and discrete.

Spoke continued, "We would be inserted at 2200 at Tay Ninh. We move to a point northwest of the city. It would be about 2 hours overland to Xa Dao Ninh, the target, after we get across the Mekong River. Once there, we remain together. At sunrise, we circle the village, taking whatever pics we need as well as draw maps of whatever will be useful. There is a slight rise here (he said pointing at the map). We wait until dark and then move back to Tay Ninh together.

"From 2330 tonight, we have scripted radio traffic giving the world our plan to move against Xa Vo Dat eighty miles northeast of Tay Ninh and almost 100-miles opposite the intended target.

"The CINCPACFLT rep said he'd have Marine assets at Bien Hoa and Bao Loc provide increased radio signals pointing to an immanent attack near Xa Vo Dat using assets from Da Lat and Nha Trang. With enough "dropped signals" even Hanoi would believe there was going to be an all-out offensive going down there.

"We would need to mobilize the rest of our team to go for a short helo ride and shopping trip to Nha Trang dropping us off at Tay Ninh and then on to Nha Trang. The NVA will think we are feinting to Tay Ninh and really be heading to Nha Trang."

Bee stood watching with a smile coming across his face. "Did you do this much planning because you thought you were going with us? Or are you still thinking outside the box?"

"No, Sir. I felt that whoever went on this op needed every advantage possible since we had relatively little info on the area and we would be in Cambodia. The fact that it is this close to Tay Ninh and has not been closely monitored really concerns me. Are those Army pukes that stupid?" asked Spoke.

Tay Ninh was one of the largest forward-deployed helo bases in South Vietnam and just north of the infamous Parrot's Beak. It was operated by the Army as well as South Vietnamese Rangers. The real question was why this target was so critically close to an Army base and not discovered.

"Keep in mind that some are less worried about the whole. They just want to do their time here and go home. That goes for any branch, even us. Now judging from the first couple of ops you designed, I think you're right. You're really ready to be a member of this observation team. Alright, let's find out what's so special about this place."

Bee called in the rest of the team. "We'll be traveling light this time. Spoke, Mitchell, Goetz and me. The rest of the team will go for a ride to Tay Ninh and then on to Nha Trang. You are the smoke and mirrors. We get dropped off at Tay Ninh. Radio chatter will place the flight and you as a diversion for the Nha Trang area. You merely go up, take in a few beers at the club, go shopping and wait 'til dark and come home. We'll see you here in a couple of days."

Senior Chief LaMonde piped up, "What's to say? Some of us have to make sacrifices for the good of the team. Get geared up, gents! We're going shopping!"

CHAPTER 8 – PEEKING UNDER THE TENT

Near Xa Dao Ninh on the Cambodian border

It was raining again. Not the hard, wind-driven monsoon rains, but the constant warm, drizzle-type rains so common to this region. The jungle dripped incessantly long after the actual rain stopped. The heat didn't help. It made your clothing seem to crawl not to mention the insects that always sensed when you were supposed to be absolutely still. It must be a pheromone or something that they sensed when you could not swat them, thought Spoke.

Spoke thanked God and his genetics that mosquitoes and other insect bites did not seem to bother him. It bothered him to get bit, of course, but no welt and no residual scratching.

The smells were the oppressively humid assault on nasal passages. It was the same smell just before the rain started, but horribly more stagnant and hot; smells of rotting vegetation, rotting garbage, ozone mixed with methane, stagnant body odor, human and animal feces and urine.

The up-side was that sunrise was due in the next hour and that would make things light enough for pictures even though it was overcast. The down-side was that the heat would only magnify the smells and rancid odors of the village – rancid that is until your nose and senses became desensitized. All the team had to do was just wait.

They'd humped it for six miles in the dark after making a night-time crossing of the Mekong River. Now they just had to be patient.

Spoke needed no reminder that the game and the bullets were real. His adrenal glands were working overtime.

The unit members spaced themselves within 10 yards of each other. Spoke was second from the end. He needed to move closer. He carefully signaled Bee. He needed the cover of foliage to get closer to the buildings. The plan was to move quietly around the perimeter of the village and observe, taking pictures as needed and sketching items of interest that couldn't be properly photographed. The key was not being seen or getting caught. Cover and concealment seemed easy enough. The jungle provided plenty of cover.

Concealment, however, from local animals seemed more of a challenge. The few dogs weren't as troublesome as the monkeys and birds. The double and triple canopy gave them places to hide and the noise factor was unusually bothersome due to the heavy air and reflective nature of the foliage.

Spoke thought that if he was to ever get a guard dog, monkeys would far surpass even the rowdiest dog. He was familiar with geese and their ability to warn as well as be attack animals, but he thought monkeys would be even better. As a kid on his grandparents' farm, he'd encountered geese. They were nothing to mess with either.

Daylight sounds overcame night sounds. The overlap was noticeable, and expected. What wasn't expected was the roar of a tiger in the jungle. Great, thought Bee, as if he didn't have enough concerns with a newbie, now he had a tiger nearby.

Spoke moved softly through the jungle undergrowth. His heartbeat was so loud, he was sure he'd be discovered with that alone, never mind his camera. He'd chosen a Minolta SRT-101 body with a 200mm/ f5.6 lens. It was lighter and had an even better light-metering system than his Nikon F-1. The most important thing was that it was quieter than the Nikon. The Minolta still made the characteristic metallic sound of a single lens reflex, but it was better than anything else he had. He felt he needed every advantage. To the team, he gave the impression he was ready for anything. In reality he was scared beyond imagination. Training could only go so far. These bullets were very real and the men using them wanted his life as much as he did.

He waited for some background noise and took his first 'happy snap', the prime ingress road to the village. Actually, truth be told, it was really an enlarged rutted trail. In his mind, the question became why was this quiet little village so important and why were there so many people milling around when obviously the housing situation didn't seem to match?

The high point near the village could not have been more than 80 feet above the floor of the surrounding jungle. On the map, the contour lines showed a slight depression and then a rise, but the map didn't really show the correct contour lines. That was part of the reason they were there. Something had to be clarified and determined as to what this village included.

He moved to his left and took another picture. As he listened to the sounds, he became more confident in his position and his abilities. He began to work more independently from the rest of the team. As he continued to move, he almost forgot they were there. Soon he was out-maneuvering his cover – a major rookie mistake.

His attention was focused on a small group of men. He watched them head off on a path almost hidden from the village. He started to follow when one of the men stopped and turned back to the village. Spoke froze. Sounds of the monkeys increased as if someone threw something at them. It was a danger call. The jungle seemed to go crazy. The man returning to the village looked up. Spoke moved at the same time.

Spoke ducked and went to his knees. He laid down and slid into position. The mud seemed to make the landing much easier.

What was that smell?! Spoke rolled over quietly, focusing on the intruder not 25 feet away. The man continued to head over to his apparent lodging. Spoke lay still. What the heck was that smell?

The monkeys and birds started again with new vigor. It gave him the chance to move. Where did the team go? Spoke moved toward the trail. He still had pictures to take. He was sure the team was close and watching him. They were professional even if he wasn't.

He moved quickly to the trail. It was well used and obviously led somewhere. Noise from the trail stopped him. He froze. Then silently and quickly he moved into the foliage.

Three men came down the trail walking toward the village huts. Spoke watched as they continued laughing and talking. The other man came out of the hut and started running down the trail passing within 15 feet of Spoke. He was so preoccupied with being late to whatever he was late for, that he didn't even consider he was being watched. Where was he going in such a hurry?

This was all he could stand. Spoke had to follow the clue. He had to find out what was so important about this village. He moved back from the trail. The next people down the trail might not be so preoccupied.

Spoke moved as silently as conditions allowed through the jungle. Soft rain started again. Still no sign of the team. He sheltered his camera and carefully kept moving through the jungle. That smell still seemed to be around. Damn, whatever it was, it sure stank.

The noise that alerted Spoke didn't sound like monkeys, birds or anything wild. The yell was angry and obviously directed at someone or something derelict in its function or duty or out of fear. Spoke wished he could understand them, but the tone of the voice alone crossed all barriers of language or culture. It was mad and fearful at the same time. The response was absolutely furious.

Suddenly there was a burst of gunfire. The birds and monkeys went crazy. What followed was almost a cheer from a group of men. Excitedly the group talked all at once.

Moving toward the sound, Spoke had to find out what was there. The undergrowth began thinning. Then it opened up creating a clearing. He squatted down and hid. His camera came up. That's what was so important about this place.

Quickly he snapped several pictures as the normal jungle sounds began to return. Did he dare move past the site and get more? He waited totally absorbed in the sight before him. With the double and triple canopy, overhead viewing was not possible. Ground photos were essential.

Suddenly he was startled into reality with a very subtle sound. He felt the ice-cold fear of the discovered. His eyes must have bulged out of his head. He knew he screwed up. He froze and realized he had been way too cavalier with his anonymity. What was he thinking?

Almost completely silent was the whispered inquiry, "What stinks?" Bee moved almost effortlessly forward out of the rain-soaked foliage.

Spoke smiled a wan smile and turned back towards the clearing. He did not want the fear in his eyes to give away his horrified feelings.

Ahead both men looked incredulously at the sight before them. Not 30 yards away was a group of men digging footings. A makeshift wheelbarrow with bags of cement was sheltered from the dripping foliage with large palm fronds. Nine other men were digging a trench while one stood holding a huge King Cobra. The cobra was obviously filled with bullet holes and the men still were talking about it.

The footings were virtually unnecessary for normal jungle dwellings. All the huts in the village were on stilts and built off the ground for multiple reasons. One of those reasons was being held in their hands.

The lower area closer to the river did have occasional flooding but this particular site was on a rise. Footings rather than pilings implied something far more permanent and problematic.

The split bamboo 'piping' led to specific locations around the footings. Pictures could not explain it all. Drawings were needed to show what could not be 'said with a thousand words.' They were not drainage pipes. Conduits like that could be for wiring or water supplies, but why water? No, it had to be for wiring. OK, but for what? Let's get home alive and do the evaluation later, Spoke thought.

One of the men shouted at the workers to work harder and protect the bags of cement. He had a North Vietnamese Army Officer's uniform. The realization that the NVA did not have any consideration for national boundaries came quickly back to mind.

With the pictures and the drawings completed, both Spoke and Bee carefully moved back into the very dense undercover foliage. Quietly they moved to an obviously predetermined place. Spoke followed Bee and emulated his every move. Slowly, inexorably slowly, they moved back almost to their starting location. The rain began again, this time in earnest. This probably would mean the end of work on whatever project they were performing. Now they waited.

It didn't take long for the other two SEALS to arrive. "What's that smell? It smells like shit!" Goetz complained softly. All quietly nodded in agreement.

The rain continued. Dinner time came and the darkness seemed to envelop them. C-rats were the order of the day. They might have been good once upon a time, but the Korean War dates stamped on the cans still did not improve the taste of anything.

Sounds of the day evolved into the sounds of night. The roar in the distance was the roar of a hungry tiger. The monkeys responded, but without the bitter antagonizing screams from earlier. Seems all was quiet except for the rain. The endless drone of mosquitoes accompanied the sheltered men as they tried to sleep or at least snooze under the semi-protection of the broad-leafed jungle plants.

Time finally came to get out of there. Other than the few calls of nature, they'd laid quietly in the wet undergrowth waiting for the welcome blanket of total darkness.

At about 2000, the men shook off the stiffness they'd endured. Quietly they used the dripping of the leaf canopy to mask their egress. They still required some 8 hours to get back to Tay Ninh with the raw intelligence that would hopefully shed light on the importance of that village and site. This was more than enough time, but the route was in "injun territory." It also meant another wet crossing of the Mekong.

Each was wet to the skin. The still, warm night air made it seem like they were wearing Lycra body suits, only these suits didn't give or move freely. Moving through the jungle, the only sounds were the occasional sound of metal fittings on their weapons and canteen covers. They were all dog-tired.

They'd spent serious time getting a look at something that didn't belong there, something that was important enough to pique the attention of MACV and CINCPACFLT. Whatever it was, it had to have some very important meaning.

Arrival at Tay Ninh was uneventful albeit long and wet. The actions of the day finally were taking the edge off the adrenaline rush of the entire experience. To Spoke, the adrenaline rush had long ago been passed by the roar of screaming limbs and exhausted breathing still in his ears. But Spoke felt he had to keep it to himself. He had the greatest feelings of admiration for these men and the team as a whole. He would not let it be known he was a complainer. Without the actual experience, a person could never know.

His plan for Major Big Red had already begun. Now it was his turn to spring the trap and collect his extra dessert.

Once back at Tay Ninh, they would have to wait until first light for the helo ride home, but at least they were in friendly territory, safe as any other place in South Vietnam.

The night continued to drag on. Finally, the enveloping clouds of night seemed to lift with the gradual first light of a new day. Clamoring aboard their designated chariot of the skies, they all eased into web seats and strapped in.

The flight from Tay Ninh seemed amazingly short, probably because Spoke slept. Arriving at the military side of Saigon's Tan Son Nhut Air Base, the small team headed for the flight ops shack. Entering, the duty officer looked at the drenched men, "What the hell is that smell? Someone shit their pants? Or did one of you get into tiger shit? One of our pilots did the same thing after an ejection a few months ago."

All the men looked at each other. Spoke looked at his pants. That was it. When he slid into the jungle, he'd slid into the toilet of a tiger. He knew he'd never live this one down.

MACV Headquarters, Saigon, Republic of South Vietnam

Spoke and Bee were standing again in the huge vault where the Intelligence Center was located, but this time in the Photographic Interpretation (PI) section. Each looked almost unbelievingly at the photos and film on the light table. Spoke had provided two rolls of 35mm film that were amazingly detailed. Coupled with his drawings, it became evident what they were looking at. The foundations were oriented in a type of circular pattern with the bamboo conduits leading to a central location adjacent to the rough circle where the cement foundation was being created.

This meant only one of two things. Hidden by the triple canopy of the foliage, an anti-aircraft gun emplacement or SA-2 site. The rise adjacent to the probable weapon site had a flat bunker-like revetment for the corresponding radar.

The SA-2, or "flying telephone pole," was a surface to air guided missile that continued to bring down many aircraft in the Vietnamese conflict.

It had not been used effectively against fast, low-flyers like helicopters, not impossible mind you, just less than effective.

Comparing the data before them with the latest info from other intelligence centers out of theater, a potentially critical piece of intelligence was unfolding. It appeared the site could be an anti-aircraft gun emplacement, possibly even a radar guided weapon system – a Russian ZSU-type system – a first for this area. But why there? Was there something they had not seen?

Also, since it was officially in Cambodia, it was technically out of reach of U.S. military personnel. At least that was what the North Vietnamese hoped would happen. The North Vietnamese soldiers and Viet Cong didn't care. International borders were only an issue for U.S. forces. That left South Vietnamese forces to possibly do the heavy lifting. Tay Ninh, after all, was a South Vietnamese Special Warfare base.

Once the guns and radar systems were installed and operational, the triple canopy foliage and trees would be removed at the last minute and the site would be activated. The possible shoot-down of helos from Tay Ninh loomed very strong. What would entice helos to go into Cambodia? Maybe there really was something bigger they had not seen.

With some pin-point aerial support, the site could never become active, but it would require knowing when the weapons had reached their emplacement in order for them to be destroyed and not diverted to another location.

Bee and Spoke both knew it would require another op back to Xa Dao Ninh to call in the air strike. Since they already lifted the edge of the tent, the camel could poke his nose inside whenever they wanted.

Since SEAL Team had already been there, it was logical and probable that they would return. The assignment conflict would be centered on the needs of CINCPACFLT and MACV. It really was up to the "elephants" and both Spoke and Bee were glad they didn't have to dance with them. It was why the big boys got paid the big bucks.

CHAPTER 9 – THE LOVE CONNECTION

Officers Club, MACV, Saigon, Republic of South Vietnam

The noise inside the club was gradually increasing as more men and women from MACV and surrounding commands as well as "permitted escorts" drifted in. It was readily apparent which of the Eurasian women were military and who were not. The well-shaped bodies and well-manicured hands of the civilians easily stood out against the "sturdy" looking women from the Army, Navy and Air Force. Some of the Navy nurses there were really good looking, but most were married. Still many of them were not averse for a non-encumbered relationship be it short-termed or one-night stands.

Spoke stood to the side of the bar with Bee. Spoke had his San Miguel Ginger Ale and Bee his favorite, Johnny Walker Black Label straight up. Bee was looking for a target. He had already expressed to Spoke that if he got lucky, don't wait up for him.

Bee had been married but it had ended two years ago. Too much time away from the home fires for her and too little time for them to bond and be faithful. Bee had turned inward and focused his frustration on his work. He'd volunteered for more and more combat duty assignments. He'd been rewarded by rapidly advancing the ladder of rank and privilege.

His previous wife wanted little to do with him and had remarried within three months of their divorce. Since there were no children, he had no alimony or child support and had all of his pay and allowances as well as hazardous duty pay and tax-free status for being in a combat zone. He was not hurting for ready cash, but still felt the pain and loneliness of no love in his life. Most of his pay went to an account in the states, and when he retired, he knew he'd have more than enough to live well on.

As both men turned from the bar, an apparently misplaced young lady walked in. She was a brunette and had dark flashing eyes. She looked out of place and more than a little lost. Several Navy nurses called out to her. She smiled and walked over to them. Bee noted that she wasn't wearing a wedding ring but did have a tasteful choice of jewelry adorning her slender form.

Bee turned to Spoke and quietly stated flatly, "I think I'm in love." He smiled and turned toward the group of nurses. Carefully, he walked over to them.

Another young man, obviously interested, headed toward the group as well. Arriving first, Bee asked if he could interest her in a drink. She smiled and said simply, "Thank you."

The obviously late interloper arrived and also invited her to his table with his other companions. She looked at Bee and then turned to the other young man and politely stated she was being entertained by Bee. Perhaps another time.

Bee was extremely taken with her in a big way and felt stirrings deep within his being. The other nurses in the group smiled and one winked at her, encouraging her to have fun. She reached up and hooked her arm through his and allowed him to lead her toward where Spoke and he had been standing.

"I'm Lieutenant Commander Randy Rogers. My friends call me Bee. Please just don't call me "Late for Supper." Bee's feeble attempt at humor did not go unappreciated, however.

Sandy smiled and chuckled.

"I don't believe I've seen you here before," Bee continued.

"I'm Lieutenant Sandra Morse. My friends call me Sandy. I just arrived yesterday from Balboa Naval Hospital in San Diego. I'm afraid I'm still getting my feet on the ground here," she replied simply. She obviously had no pre-conceived notions about meeting people here in a combat theater. Most of the other nurses came with their armor and guards up. She seemed so innocent.

"Where do you hail from?" Bee asked.

"I'm from a lot of different places. I was a Navy brat. Most of my growing up time was spent all over the world," she stated again simply.

She looked directly into his eyes. She was really beautiful and he realized he was sliding quickly into a deep abyss. The thing that really surprised him was he wanted to slide.

Bee went on, "I am assuming you are a Navy nurse."

Sandra replied, "Yes and have been for 6 years. Where are you assigned?"

Bee wanted to open up and tell her everything, but he recognized this was probably a frustrated response from an equally frustrated desire to be with her. His measured response simply stated that he was with CINCPACFLT. Then he focused his own "attack" on where she was staying and what her duty assignments were. He found out she was being assigned to the burn trauma unit, doing much as she'd done in San Diego.

Bee thought, someone with this kind of inner strength had to have tremendous 'self-image stock'. He knew he wanted to see her more. He felt a certain struggling within himself to express those feelings, but also felt restrained, after all he'd only just met her.

The local band in the adjacent ballroom started their next set and Bee looked at Spoke. The message in the look was "See you later. Don't worry, I'll be alright." It was the covert signal similar to the collegiate necktie hung over the door knob. Simply stated it said, "Occupied. Don't come in, or even think of knocking."

Spoke knew that look, but thought Bee really wouldn't be alright. He covertly winked and turned back to his ginger ale. Bee started to escort his new-found friend toward the dance floor. Spoke knew he would have to find another ride back home.

Seeing the team's XO, "Swede" Swolchowski, Spoke nodded to Bee and tossed him the keys to the Jeep. "Be careful and don't get lost," he smiled and walked toward the other group who were getting louder with each round purchased.

"XO," smiled Spoke. "Seems the boss may be getting lucky. You need a designated driver?"

"Shhurr," replied Swede smiling. It was obvious that Happy Hour had not been wasted on him. Now it was up to Spoke to navigate him to their Jeep before any displays of overt manliness began and forced an unscheduled sightseeing side-trip to the brig. Swede had always been a happy drunk, unlike some of the other members of the team.

Spoke began first by asking for the keys. Swede unsteadily handed them to him. Spoke then gently reminded Swede to use the 'head' before he made a fool of himself.

Swede smiled and nodded. Swede turned and slowly, shakily, made his way through the crowd toward the Men's Room. Several of their group called out to him and said he didn't need to leave yet; the party was just starting.

Spoke smiled back at them and said, "He'll be back." What he didn't say was that he'll be back another day and another time. Then he headed off to guide the XO to their ride home.

CHAPTER 10 – CUPID'S ARROW HITS ITS MARK

MACV Officer's Club, Saigon

Bee felt a magnetism he'd thought he'd never feel again. He was so taken with Sandy that he could hardly keep his wits about him. He'd only had half of one drink, but Sandy had caused a buzz in his head like a sawmill. It appeared she seemed to feel the same way. Was it the animal magnetism frequently expressed and encountered in a war zone, or was this really something far deeper?

He kept saying to himself to keep it light. This was no time to get involved. He'd heard of guys that had let all their past be known and how they really felt, not to mention left their guard down. It seemed that somehow it never worked out. Worse yet, come to find out the other person ended up involved with someone back home or were married. He really didn't want this to happen to him. He'd watched how such experiences had devastated individuals even to their demise.

Sandy snuggled closer to him in the embrace of his arms as they started to dance. The music swirling in her ears and mind. She'd left a boyfriend, Robert, in San Diego who'd come home from Vietnam badly burned from a napalm attack that got too close to friendly troops – friendly fire literally. She felt that he was dependent on her and the six-month affair was more of the patient-nurse kind of love rather than the deep sense of inner love. This man that held her was not that way at all. She sensed he had strong feelings toward her already. Was that just because she was a long way from the safety of the States, or was it because it was something really real?

Carefully they danced over to a darker part of the floor. He was humming with the music. She felt the emergence of feelings growing within her. His embrace, his airs, his warmth, just everything about him. The manly muskiness of his body, the moistness of his hands, all surrounded her with an intense, palpable feeling of willingness to succumb to both of their feelings.

Suddenly Robert and San Diego were a galaxy away. She knew it wasn't the alcohol. She'd only had a sip of one white wine. She'd had a lot more than this before and still hadn't felt this way. The room was swirling.

Her eyes closed and she felt his protective comfort. She was safe here; she was where she really wanted to be. Robert was only a far-away fling a lifetime ago. This had the makings of a real love affair.

More questions crept into her mind. Was he married? Was there someone else? Was he just using her for a one-night stand? She needed to keep her guard up, but how? He totally seemed to dominate her very being. She seemed to know him from somewhere else. But, how?

Bee held her close. Her faintly subtle perfume was driving him crazy. The scent of her hair and her smooth hands. Her warmth. Her willingness to fall into his arms. Her supple body pressing close. The compression of her body into his. He wanted to tell her everything about his past, about his failed marriage, about everything he hoped for, about everything he dreamed of. Still those nagging questions in his mind. Was she involved with someone else? Was she married? Was he headed for a train wreck? Was he just to be a one-night stand? She felt so wonderful and so...... so right.

The music ended. They continued to hold on to each other. The fact that another couple bumped them as they passed didn't seem to matter. Finally, they stopped. He smiled sheepishly at her and she returned the smile. He reached down with his right hand, brushing her warm body. She grabbed his hand pressed it to her asking quietly if he would be willing to take her home; she'd had too much excitement for one night. Maybe it was still jet-lag but she was feeling really vulnerable.

He stopped almost in mid-heartbeat. Had he upset her? Was she just tired or was she inviting him home? How could he read this beautiful woman; the first woman he'd actually felt desire for in too long a time. Maybe it really was jet-lag. After all she'd just traveled over half a world away and only had a day to recover. He toned down his hormones. That must be it. She was just tired.

He smiled and said he'd be happy to get her to her room. The dreamy look in her eyes gave everything away. That look often followed one too many, or someone really tired and bent on hitting the rack. He led her from the room and through the bar. The other nurses watched in amazement as the two of them left. The rowdy group drinking their frustrations away yelled and whistled at him. He ignored them focusing on the critical op at hand.

He headed for his Jeep. Arriving, he lifted her into the passenger seat. She smiled and leaned over and kissed his cheek. It stopped him cold. He wanted to return the kiss, but held off. Was this a come-on? Was she signaling that she wanted more? Or was she just being nice and saying "Thanks." This was not going to be it, was it?

She was tired, but not that tired. She was really falling, but not so much that she knew where and what she was doing. The kiss was an invitation. It was a calculated risk she wanted to take. She wanted him unlike anyone she'd ever wanted before. She held her emotions in check, however. She had to find out more about him, yet she could have sworn that she'd known him all her life. Was this even possible? Was she headed for a heart-breaking experience? What was happening to the suave, gentle woman that always held everything at bey, controlling the scene; controlling the situation; controlling her emotions?

She quietly said she was living at the Navy Nurse's Barracks by the hospital. She lived on the second floor, room 206.

Starting the Jeep, he drove carefully toward the hospital. He didn't want to arouse any suspicions from the MP's. After all, he'd only had part of a drink. Any other inebriation was caused by the young lady next to him. Arriving at the barracks a few minutes later, he pulled into a parking place. Getting out, he walked around to her side to be the gentleman he really was. She again placed her arm on his shoulder and leaned over and kissed him again, this time on the lips. It was a gentle kiss, but with that act, the dam burst. The next kiss was anything but gentle. There was nothing but all-out emotion. She came up for air and whispered that she really wanted to have him with her tonight.

CHAPTER 11 – THE TRAP WORKS

The weekend had been much needed for all of the men. Everyone on the team knew the skipper was 'tracking a target.' From the bounce in his step to the twinkle in his eye, everything he said and did screamed 'I'm back on track – target acquired.' Several winked and smiled at the 'new skipper.'

At his makeshift desk, Spoke studied the list of assignments from MACV. Big Red was back to his old form. One of the assignments on the list intrigued him as he studied the target folders. Since his initial tangle with LaRose's office over target folders, suddenly lots of information accompanied all requests for assignments given to SEAL Team. At least they wouldn't be going back to Xa Dao Ninh, or as some on the team quipped, 'tiger shit alley' any time soon. The long range recon teams from the South Vietnamese Rangers would get that opportunity and the glory for that mission, thanks to SEAL Team One, Det B.

The rumor mill, known as scuttlebutt in the Navy and Marine Corps, around MACV was Big Red had been dressed down by the General for some very 'shoddy work.' It appeared the representative for CINCPACFLT did have some pull with "Inner Sanctum."

Rumor also had it that he was soon heading for another less taxing assignment in a much, much colder climate: something about a radar picket station in northern Alaska. Would wonders ever cease? Spoke thought about his call to CINCPACFLT just prior to the last mission. Big Red could never have seen that one coming. Now when would he get that extra dessert and the star on his forehead?

Smiling, he noted this particular assignment was not as spectacular as what was in the target folder. It appeared to be just a simple recon of a village gone to the other side, 'a look and see,' but there was something much more intriguing about the location and the layout of the village. Why weren't there more huts, and why weren't there more people. It just didn't look right.

Could it be the depth of the double and triple canopy jungle, or maybe the proximity to the river, or even the minimal smoke rising from any cooking fires. Things just didn't add up. The photo's time and date stamp in the corner should have clearly shown more smoke from the huts, even just a few huts.

Spoke called Bee and together they looked at the anomaly before them. Both looked at each other and Bee agreed. It wasn't all it was cracked up to be. Their plan had to make sure that what they were to do and what looked like should be done were both covered.

"Are you ready to help us with another look-see?" he asked Spoke.

"Yes, Sir," came the eager reply.

"Let's get a plan together and we'll see what is bothering both of us about this place."

Spoke started into the target folder. First of all, it was in Laos. Recently, they'd been given sanction to pursue locations contributing to the war efforts farther north along the Ho Chi Minh Trail. Already the team had been in Laos on interdiction operations. As a side note, they'd uncovered narcotics trafficking and production sites.

Was this one of those situations? Spoke called the CINCPACFLT rep in Saigon. He'd needed everything possible on this location – friendly villages, supply points, possible narcotics production sites and so forth. He asked if they had any maps or photos that had not been passed to MACV. Since this was a long-range op, he also requested a reconnaissance photo mission of the area. While still in its early development, giant-scale photos would be appreciated too.

Giant-scale meant satellite photos. Unlike later years, this took dedicated assets to be tasked weeks and in some cases months in advance. Since they did not have that kind of time, he would have to rely on past photos and archived missions from long ago. These were still Top Secret and were used on a need-to-know basis. He needed them and definitely knew about them from his activities with CINCPACFLT in Hawaii.

Fortunately, Commander Lutz in Saigon knew of Spoke's pedigree both with CINCPACFLT and in his own family. He had admired the young Lieutenant and his lineage. He also knew ADM Donophan like this young man. He had to keep the boss happy.

Within two days, Spoke had what he needed. His call to CINCPACFLT Hawaii also generated some excellent support. He had not gone around the local CINCPACFLT rep, CDR Lutz. He'd kept him in the loop using his friends in the Intelligence Center at CINCPACFLT. This had been met with appreciation due to the fact that he'd also given extra credit to CDR Lutz in Saigon. Spoke knew how to stroke his friends and build their reputations too.

After looking carefully at the packages that arrived, Spoke called Bee in and proposed a solution to the long-range concept of operations. The logistics of this kind of operation definitely required a larger team effort. In fact, it may require an extended period of time in Laos.

This meant living off the land. Most of the Hmong villages in Laos not only would help the team, but provide lodging and support too. Spoke was to meet another asset of the team, the Hmong. True, weapons and ammunition would be traded for their help as well as remuneration from the U.S. government, but this was an all-out push to help the good guys win.

If this was a narcotics mill or trans-shipment site, the Hmong were just as supportive of stopping it as though the plague of drugs were their own issue, never mind the world's.

The Hmong also were in the sights of the North Vietnamese and Viet Cong. Numerous attacks on Hmong villages using chemical weapons and gasses had left the Hmong as sworn enemies of the North Vietnamese. The pro-North Vietnamese backed Communist Pathet Lao and Royal Laotian military had turned a blind eye when the atrocities against the Hmong occurred. The only friend the Hmong seemed to have was the U.S.

How much they would be given or recompensed was handled at a higher level. All Spoke and Bee needed to know was that they could count on Hmong friendlies being ready to help.

With that in hand, the plan quickly came together.

CHAPTER 12 – THE CRIES OF BABES

37 miles from Muang Sing, Laos, on the Nam Loi River

It was like every other day in Laos, indeed in almost all of Southeast Asia, the air was hot and seemed to weigh a ton. Everything just seemed to radiate intense, humid pressure. And it was wet. So wet and heavy that the weight seemed to press everything down – clothes, hair, leaves, grass. It was dead quiet and dead calm. Not a sound in the double canopy, monkeys or even birds. The ambient pressure even seemed to make all sound fall to the ground. Smells, normally assaulting the human olfactory senses now reflected more of their own personal hygiene or lack thereof. Sweat and their two-day unbathed body odor seemed to insult rather than assault their senses.

Spoke knew the men they watched were talking out loud and not whispering, but he couldn't make out what they were saying and yet they were only 20 or so yards away. He was sure he could walk around whistling and no one would be the wiser much less care.

Bee lay quietly in his ghillie suit about 10 feet from Spoke, sweat dripping down his nose and smarting his eyes. SEALS were extensively trained on how to construct indigenous camouflage outfits starting with a basic mesh garment, yarn and local vegetation and to do it in less than 30 minutes. Bee had excelled at this training. He seemed to have a knack, even a talent, for making these critical pieces of equipment. At Sniper School, he'd been so good that an instructor had walked up to within six feet of him without seeing him. That was then, he was here and now.

Bee watched the three men mill around the shack smoking and talking. The bitter smoke from their Chinese cigarettes seemed to hang around their bodies giving them an almost ethereal look. Each one barely moved and carrying their weapons appeared to be an unusual burden. One rifle even rested against the owner's leg.

The AK-47 looked worn and badly in need of attention. Spots of rust on the barrel and receiver-cover demonstrated the abject reliability of this weapon. It had been demonstrated for over 20 years. They knew the weapon would always shoot no matter what. His magazine was rusted and Bee was more than grateful his M-14 was far better taken care of.

Bee was also glad he could opt out of those new plastic M-16s. Cleaning the stupid gas tube had been the downfall of many a jammed weapon. Soldiers crawling through rice paddies with excessively dirty powder residue build-ups in the tubes spelled one jam after another and usually only at the wrong time. It also spelt the all too frequent death of the user. Still, some of the team had become attached to the short CAR-15 version and its miniscule cartridge. They claimed the extra rounds they could carry more than compensated for the other issues. Bee was of the old school that professed one shot/one kill. Why carry all the extra rounds when they could have carried extra water instead?

The team watched as the sun seemed to freeze into position. Just a breeze would have been nice. Even a bird flying by might have moved the air enough to give the sensation of air movement.

This op required that the team wait until 1800 hours and observe all activity coming and going from the shacks. Then they were to move far enough away to regroup and position themselves for their evening activity, a barn burning and personnel snatch.

The scene before them at the edge of the village included an elevated thatch-roofed house as well as the three guards. The folliage was cleared some 75 feet from the shack walls, but already he could see that the jungle was doing its best to recapture its lost area.

An almost imperceptible movement caught Spoke's eye. A small python-like snake seemed to move the grass with the patient movement of a killer on the prowl. Its tongue flicked noiselessly but it definitely had a small rodent in mind for dinner.

The only thing any of the team had seen all afternoon was one guard talking to another and a third take a leak at the edge of the hut's clearing. Spoke was also feeling the need to relieve himself. He watched as the three men entered the shack as three more replaced them. Whatever was in there, it appeared it was worth at least six men's lives – very much the chance that it was a newly placed Viet Cong leader.

Overhead images had previously confirmed this was supposed to be one of a myriad of huts possibly a transshipment location; drugs, contraband, ammo, etc. It was only two hundred yards from the Nam Loi River, but might as well have been 200 miles. An almost completely overgrown path went through the jungle to the shacks and clearing. On the other side of the stream was the densest double canopy jungle Bee could ever remember seeing.

Last week's latest enhanced imagery clearly showed that it was still active. Signs on the river clearly showed that small liter boats had been using the site for shipments of semi-finished heroin bales from the highlands of China and other areas of the Golden Triangle. If there were more bales in the shack, or if they were waiting for more bales, then those six guards were preparing to take the cargo farther down-stream and possibly more small shipments as well. His team's op was to confirm that, but just how much, if any, was the real million-dollar question. More importantly, what could they do about it?

Capturing and taking the village chief would also help to answer questions left unanswered. There was the possibility that it was arms and ammunition being transferred here. While pretty far-fetched, it still was possible, thought Spoke.

Spoke gently moved his hand to his side. Chao Lis, "Chewy" to his American associates, their Hmong guide on this operation seemed to sense the slight brush of the hand and quietly opened his eyes. Spoke motioned gently that he had to relieve himself. He signaled his intent along with information about what was happening and more importantly what was not happening.

Chewy carefully and deliberately rolled from his back to an alert position. His rolling motion was as quiet and stealthy as the python had been. He watched intently at the shack and three men.

Many field operatives seemed to develop a sixth sense about others watching them. The guards obviously were more muscle than brains and definitely were not trained. They sensed nothing.

Timing his movements, Spoke headed surreally away from Chewy without even stirring the still air. One of the guards had the same idea and wandered over to the edge of the jungle.

Relieved, some four minutes later, Spoke motioned with his eyes to the far side of the shack. Shouting voices came from inside and then out came five more guards. They muttered something to the remaining guard inside and then 8 men headed for the jungle trail. Not three, not six, but eight men. There had to be something really important in that shack.

Chewy signaled Bee that there must be at least 10, one inside and one now outside plus the 8 headed for the river. This load was definitely not just another small load of drugs or even guns.

Almost imperceptibly at first, a gentle breeze began in the top canopy of trees. As if on cue, birds and monkeys came to life calling and moving slightly at first, but more rapidly as the breeze seemed to pick up. While not a strong breeze, at least there was cover and movement sounds to break the monotony.

The guard at the shack looked around but mostly focused on the jungle trail. He obviously was not a trained operator. He leaned his gun down against the shack and picked up a small pebble. Looking at it, he threw it. Then he repeated the exercise oblivious to the personal danger only feet from him.

The door opened suddenly and another guard came out and yelled at the outside guard. It was apparent that he was upset that the guard did not have his weapon in his hands. He ordered him to trade places with him and to keep his eyes open in case the rest of the group came back. Once they'd traded places, the second guard headed over to the jungle edge and urinated like he had been holding it for days.

Finished and much more relaxed, he began looking into the jungle. He strained as if to see whatever it was that caught his attention. Looking around, he carefully entered the jungle with his weapon at the ready. Momentarily he disappeared. Bee, Spoke and Chewy struggled also to see, but the jungle was so dense there was no way to see anything. Had they been discovered? Discovered by a rank amateur?

All men went to high alert.

Bee then moved away from Chewy a couple of yards. Grateful for the breeze to cover the infinitesimal noises their position change made, they waited. Sweat streamed down their faces and continued to burn their eyes. Five minutes of hair-raising fear seemed like an eternity.

Bee reached for his knife, sensing things might get out of hand. He did not deploy it yet, but waited.

A distant rustle of leaves from the jungle trail signaled the impending return of the other 8 and more from the river. Soft voices could also be made out. Suddenly through the screen of leaves, 6 men appeared leading 11 young women all tied together and walking as if in a trance. Their clothes were nothing but rags, torn and in many cases not even covering their small, slender bodies.

Sensing something wrong, the men forced the prisoners to the ground. The bandit leader signaled one of the men to watch the girls. They started to fan out around the shack. Just at that point, the errant guard came out of the jungle pulling up his bloomer-like pants. The leader screamed at the frightened guard, leveled his AK-47 at his chest and fired. The man's sublime relief turned to immediate terror as he spun around from the shock of two 7.62x39mm rounds tearing open his chest.

It appeared like a poorly choreographed, small-budget B-grade movie. All that was needed was the Spaghetti Western music. The guard collapsed falling back. The leader screamed at the remaining men that the same fate befell them if they chose to repeat the folly of the dead guard. The girls didn't make a sound, too drugged or tired to care.

Both Bee and Chewy carefully focused on the shack. 13 men were accounted for and still vertical. Yelling at the others, the leader had

8 more guards go into the shack. They emerged with 8 more girls and forced them toward the other 11. Getting their bearings, all headed toward the river single file, the guards interspersed between the captives.

Waiting for five more minutes generated no additional guards or prisoners. Bee carefully signaled other members of the team to work forward toward the shack and then move toward the trail leading to the river.

CHAPTER 13 – HEROES PROVEN

Because this was to have been an observation op/snatch and not an interdiction, the twelve men, 10 U.S. Navy SEALs, Spoke and Chewy were to watch for their opportunity to complete the operation, not jeopardize its success by getting involved with human smugglers.

Spoke's thoughts flashed to his own personal situation. The time spent at CINCPACFLT proved invaluable. Then, just over a year later, he had been off to Vietnam. The excitement and opportunities seemed endless. He was now working with the elite warriors of the Navy. He smiled as he thought of the day when his four-year-old son came to work with him. Where he'd heard the term "Spook" was anyone's guess, but his conversation with the Admiral that day was obviously memorable. He referred to his dad's job as a "Spoke." Naturally, everyone jumped on that one and it became the nickname he was challenged with. 'Out of the mouth of babes,' he thought.

Here and now he found himself deep undercover with SEAL Team One in Laos watching members of a human smuggling group moving not only bales of raw semi-processed heroin from the poppy fields of the Golden Triangle, Burma, Laos and China, but young women. He knew these children would be sold as slaves for use in their whore operations all around the Far East or for sale to the Middle East.

Bee was absorbed watching Spoke and took his mind off the current situation for only what seemed like a second. A sudden movement and rustle of leaves, took Bee totally by surprise. One last guard at the shack had been overlooked. He stood over Bee with his AK-47 pointed at his head and chest.

How could he have been so stupid to let his mind wander? Now he, the group's leader, was the one that may compromise the whole op.

The guard was so focused on Bee that he didn't notice or hear Spoke move up behind him and quickly reach around and cover his mouth pulling him backward and off balance. Spoke's other hand held his fighting stiletto thrusting it upward through the diaphragm and into the heart of the totally surprised, wide-eyed enemy. Quickly withdrawing his knife, he slit the man's throat. Blood sprayed all over Spoke and the surrounding vegetation.

The physics was simple. The up-thrust of the stiletto forced the diaphragm to violently contract preventing any breathing. The pericardial sack surrounding the heart was ruptured forcing the heart to spasm uncontrollably and force blood to shoot into the chest cavity. The severing of the windpipe, carotid artery and jugular veins only confirmed what the first blow started.

Startled and petrified, the man was dead on his feet. He seemed to throw his rifle away trying to get away from this unseen monster that had him. He couldn't even press the trigger.

The whole evolution from discovery to dispatch lasted less than 3 seconds. Both Bee and Spoke quickly went down to their knees. Spoke remained focused on his victim, blood dripping from where the carotid artery sprayed him. Bee knew the thoughts and feelings associated with the first close combat kill he'd had and knew Spoke would need some reassurance. He also knew that he had to move his men to keep Spoke's mind off his situation.

Chewy looked in awe at Spoke. He'd also been surprised by the last guard. He realized he would be dead if Spoke had not killed the man. He also knew they had to move the team to interdict the rest of the group and slaves. Some of those girls were Hmong judging from what was left of their clothes. He had to get them back to their families.

The op? That went out the window when the last remaining guard discovered them. Besides, those young women marching by, triggered a deep, determined sadness in each man's very soul. No one at MACV said anything about drugged children. That would never happen on his watch, thought Bee, if he were running the show. Once again, Big Red had his fingerprints all over this, Bee thought.

The team mounted up and headed for routes parallel to the overgrown trail. Fortunately, the early evening increase of the wind provided enough ambient noise to mask their rapid movements through the undergrowth. The file of men and children ahead of the team also masked sounds. Monkeys and birds helped too.

The 200 yards to the river were covered in less than five minutes. The bandit group's leader stopped the file at the river and sent one of his more trusted guards to go back to the hut and get the last man.

Bee motioned Obermeyer to take care of the dispatched guard. Heading down the trail brought a surprise the man hadn't bargained for. Three minutes later, Obermeyer returned and nodded. He too was covered in blood. That guard would not be reporting either.

Meanwhile, on the side of the river there were three lashed-together wooden, raft-type boats and men were being organized to accommodate the children, bales of heroin and guards. The girls were in an obvious state of narcotic lethargy. They stumbled and whimpered.

The guards beat them with rubber hoses when they would not comply fast enough. Spoke watched with anger rising in every inch of his being.

Bee motioned for Senior Chief to move his six men around to the upstream side of the landing. They moved into position. He then motioned his men including Spoke and Chewy to get ready to stop the boats from getting into the flow of the river. The bandit leader screamed at one of his men to stop beating the child he was hitting. The man started to complain, but remembered the sight at the hut only a few minutes ago and thought better of it. Instead, he threw the child onto one of the raft-like structures with an obvious curse.

The smuggler leader then realized his other men had not returned and sounded what appeared to be an alarm. The men formed a rough perimeter at the landing and started to move away from the three rafts. Thank heavens they were not tactically efficient, thought Spoke.

With the bad guys separated from the prisoners, Senior Chief's men opened fire. Four men dropped immediately. The other six men ran for cover only to be met by Bee's crossfire. All six went down. That left the leader and one other man heading for cover.

Bee counted his men. Chewy was missing. A shot sounded twenty yards into the underbrush followed by another cry and a muffled shot. Then three more shots. Chewy moved slowly into the clearing at the landing so as not to draw fire from the SEALS. He too was covered with blood. He walked openly toward the rafts.

The children that were cognizant enough to recognize this blood-covered man walking toward them started to scream. He spoke calmly and reassuringly in Hmong to them. They started to calm down. He motioned to Bee to bring the rest of the team down. They approached Chewy. He smiled a wan smile and said they now had transportation out.

Bee nodded and smiled a sympathetic, knowing smile at Chewy. They organized how they were going to get the three rafts off and moving.

Spoke thought while not solving all the world's child slavery problems, at least these children would not be part of it.

CHAPTER 14 – HONG KONG

26 Feb 1972 – Seaward approaches to Hong Kong Harbor

It was raining, again. It had rained for the last three days.

Does the sun ever shine here? Spoke thought, silently, almost reflexively, he struggled for a grasp of the weather. The wind had also picked up and it was a cold wind. And while not a downpour, the clouds seemed to dump a non-stop outpouring of moisture. This rain was cold, not the warm rain he'd felt in Hawaii or Southeast Asia.

Newly promoted Lieutenant Marks was on Rest and Relaxation (R&R) leave after a relatively quiet five months in South Vietnam. Quiet, that is, after he'd earned his spurs on recon ops. After the first op, he'd been tasked with multiple additional "seek ops." These assignments had been with the team all over Vietnam, Cambodia and Thailand, mostly along the Ho Chi Minh Trail but had included Laos and ops farther north and west.

He'd looked forward to this trip. He'd earned it. He'd squirreled away money every chance he had. Combat pay plus specialty pay denoting his life attached to SEAL Team One, didn't seem to counter an endless need for money at home in the form of family allotments. Braces for growing, crooked teeth, glasses, other dental bills all seemed to continue regardless of his needs. All of the above kept him strapped for ready cash.

Spoke came from a long line of career Navy men. Whether his grandfather, VADM Al Marks, his dad, RADM, Kevin S. "Pappy" Marks – a Naval Aviator during WWII and Korea, or himself. He felt they knew or had known just what he was going through.

Born in Olathe, Kansas, he'd travelled all over the world as a Navy brat. His dad finally decided that he wanted to get as far from the sea as he could when he retired and chose live near Naval Air Station, Olathe, Kansas, just outside of Kansas City. Pappy seemed to be most in touch with life there. Retirement was alright, but he definitely missed the action of flying and camaraderie of his fellow aviators.

Just over a year ago his mother had passed away followed by RADM Marks a few months later. Some said when the love of his life died, Pappy seemed to lose not only his best friend, but his most trusted confident and the real will to continue.

Spoke returned to attend both funerals. As executor of his dad's estate, he stayed an additional month. He'd really grown up in that part of the world. He'd gone to the University of Kansas and graduated in Political Science. His sister Marilyn Ruth had become his best friend much to the chagrin of his wife, Charlene, who always seemed to bristle when the two women were together.

Marilyn was only 10-1/2 months younger than Kevin. Because they'd traveled all over the world as a Navy family, she'd naturally become his best friend. When problems arose, Kevin would always call Marilyn causing his wife's fits of anger. The problem with Charlene was everyone else was wrong, never her. In spite of their tempestuous marriage, they'd declared truces long enough to have two young sons and a daughter. They were all the apples of Kevin and their grandparents' eyes.

Charlene's parents had passed away just after their marriage and she never really enjoyed Kevin's parents. She said one evening in a fit of anger that she thought his parents were out to destroy their marriage. Again, everyone's wrong but me and she'd screamed that she regretted ever marrying him.

One of the parting shots Charlene's mother gave his family was to get her daughter hooked on prescription drugs, pain killers, hydrocodone and OxyContin to be specific. Yes, she went to counseling but whenever the counselor would get close to discovering what drove her to the drugs, she'd quit going. Spoke was pretty sure it was sexual abuse from either an uncle or her father, but Charlene would never talk about it.

Regardless, she refused to come to the funerals of either of her in-laws saying that the last funeral besides her own was her mother's. She'd kept that promise.

Spoke's mind closed to all the frustrating thoughts of home and focused on the present. As a Naval Intelligence Officer, his mother had counseled him to volunteer for everything. She'd never figured a life on dry ground in the field with one of the world's premier combat teams would be a consequence of being a volunteer. It did one thing, however, it forced an imposed veil of secrecy on everything and everywhere he went. This only made matters worse with his wife.

Already he'd been promoted six months early, and he'd used it to finagle a few extra side trips. This one for example. He'd already used up excess personal leave and emergency leave, but mysteriously an additional week appeared on the books along with a check from Disbursing labeled overpayment for some mysterious past bill. Knowing that he owed someone somewhere, he filed it away in his mind for another day. Why look a gift horse in the mouth? If things were not as they seemed, he'd hear about it in a few months. Not dishonest, just being a part of the Navy he'd grown up with.

Meanwhile, he was here. He'd boarded the USS Blue Ridge (LCC-19) in Keelung, Taiwan, for a short two-day hop to Hong Kong. Hong Kong was still one of the jewels of the Far East. It was where East met West... legally. Every sailor in the Far East saved up whatever they could to buy, buy, and buy. Clothes, cameras, TVs, furniture, shoes – literally everything.

Even prostitution was legal and sort of well-regulated. The idea was that doctors checked the girls and certified they were clean at least every three months. They all had to have their "blue cards" with the last check-up clearly marked on the card. Naturally the sailors not too drunk to read would look for the most recent date on the card before jumping in the sack with one. At least that was the idea.

Spoke had no interest in bringing home anything uninvited or unwelcome. As a result, he'd kept his distance from local girls and even those who were just lonely and a long way from home. In this, he often appeared cold or unapproachable. That was fine with him and he never contradicted the implication. He was as excited as all the rest of the crew and especially those in the on-board Intelligence Center.

Commander, Amphibious Forces Seventh Fleet (CTF 76) embarked aboard Blue Ridge two months before this trip. The staff Intelligence Officer, Commander Robert E. Lee Forner had achieved the reputation as a real prick. Nicknamed "the Duck," CDR Forner was a southern born and bred individual with a pronounced "short man's complex". "Duck" was the "G" rated form of the Queen Mother of all swear words that accompanied the other name the crew used behind his back, namely CDR Fornicator.

CDR Forner was a "climber" and gladly used anyone to step on to get what he wanted. Spoke was everything Duck was not. In spite of this, Duck took a liking to him. He liked Spoke's father's rank. He liked the association with individuals who had real combat experience. He liked vicariously imposing his future on men who had "been there." He'd convinced the Admiral to extend Spoke's stay in Hong Kong with additional funds to make it possible. Hence, the extra leave and the check from disbursing.

Unknown to Spoke, his name had been "volunteered" to the local office of INTERPOL as a US Navy liaison officer. The fact that INTERPOL had agents operating in Hong Kong was so hush-hush that most people had never heard of their manpower there or even the assignments they had. The reason was clear. Their charter tasked them to work with local and national police forces to stop drug trafficking as well as human trafficking. They also had a number of other duties tasking them to operate with these agencies as an advisor.

Hong Kong Rock #2 was wreaking havoc on U.S. servicemen on liberty in Hong Kong. HKR2 was pure Golden Triangle heroin cut with strychnine and powdered sugar. The product was intended to give the ultimate high quickly. Unfortunately, the concentrations of strychnine lately were often less than accurately measured due to the crude equipment used by the so-called 'pharmacists.' That meant that the batches on the street were mostly deadly.

Sailors on liberty being entertained by local call girls would have their large bankrolls removed after an altered drink or two or three followed by a slight stinging sensation as the needle went in. The unknowing serviceman then was given a trip down memory lane in some crab-infested nest. Some sailors were only fleeced and left for dead. Others were just plain dead. The chance of recovering from the stuff was about one in nine. Already there had been 21 known deaths of US servicemen in only two months.

Spoke knew stories of these girls and how persuasive they could be. Besides that, a ruthless pimp could also encourage the sailor to see things the cutie's way. As part of the Port Briefing every serviceman received prior to entering Hong Kong was the urgent requirement to travel in groups of two or more all night long. Unfortunately, the raging hormones of young men and the cockiness of invincibility driven by excess alcohol constantly clouded their judgment. After all, who wanted his buddies horning in when the young man wanted to "score." His prowess, or lack thereof, was his own business, not the rest of the ship's.

CHAPTER 15 – NEW KIND
OF ASSIGNMENT

As the CTF76 Intelligence Officer, Duck commonly threw the Admiral's two stars around freely. He caught Spoke in the passageway outside of the wardroom.

"The Admiral wants to see you on the Flag Bridge." The request was more of an order than a request and Spoke felt less than enthusiastic and more like the prisoner ordered to the gallows two days early.

Spoke really wanted this time off. His time "in country" had allowed him to save a pretty good nest egg for a wardrobe complete with silk shirts, suits, shoes as well as extras for the kids. He wanted to bring home the obligatory gifts for Charlene, the kids and Marilyn, but thought gently about that.

With this "request," Spoke felt a cold chill throughout his body. He knew CTF 76, RADM Mike "the Snake" Stewart, knew his father. They'd served in VF 121 together. Neither had expressed undying devotion to the other, and Marks had kept a low profile during the two days aboard Blue Ridge so as not to antagonize the past association with his father and family.

Marks turned to go up the ladder to the Flag Bridge without missing a step or saying a thing. The Duck followed him to ensure he "didn't get lost." Marks knew if he slowed up or even stumbled, the Duck would be an appendage resembling a tail. This he did not even want the thought of.

Upon entering the Flag Bridge, Spoke announced his presence to the Admiral. "LT Marks reporting as ordered, sir."

"Very well," the reply was neutral in tone – not condescending nor impolite – just acknowledgement.

The First Class Quartermaster standing near the chart table quietly took off his sound powered phones, headset and microphone, a shipboard device powered by the voice to other sets on the net. He then headed for the bridge wing. He'd seen the Admiral's manner before. He wasn't sure if this poor young LT was to be a guest for dinner or the dinner's main course.

The Admiral waved CDR Forner to come closer as he didn't want to say anything too loudly. The Flag Officer of the Day, CDR Rich Ellison, watched the Admiral's body language and also moved out to the opposite wing closing the door behind him.

The doors secure, the Admiral began. "I know you know me and that I served with your dad. I was sorry to hear of his passing. He had nothing but the highest of praise for you and your work ethic and devotion to the Navy and your country. Your mom as well.

"Contrary to what you might have thought or heard, we were friends. I'd flown as his wingman on numerous missions. In fact, he served on my ADM board. I know it was his personal support that got me my flag."

"Yes, sir." Spoke wanted to add that it was also his dad that had sent RADM Stewart to the Gators (Amphibious Navy) rather than a Bird Farm (aviation command or carrier wing). But that was another story for another day and another venue.

"I have a request from SECDEF through SECNAV and CINCPACFLT," he continued.

"We have a problem in Hong Kong and your unique talents are needed to help the Navy and the country. Seems there is some new kind of drug being given to our men while they are on liberty in Hong Kong. They call it Hong Kong Rock #2. It's pure heroin cut with powdered sugar and strychnine. One shot of this shit and we just lost a sailor. We need it stopped and the street sources kept away from our men. Twenty-one men have died from it in the last two months. It has to be squashed."

"What about the local police?" Spoke asked.

"Seems there are too many on the payroll of the drug Triads within the Hong Kong Police Department to trust anyone inside. We need another fresh set of eyes that will be available and functioning as a direct liaison to the Navy's NIS agents. You seem to have the best credentials for the job at this time and place. You will work with the local INTERPOL agents in Hong Kong at their request as the liaison for me, SECNAV and SECDEF. I can't tell you just how sensitive this is."

Spoke knew that few individuals knew about INTERPOL, their mission, their operational orders, or had worked with them. He knew that if the Duck knew all this, it had to have "glory by association" written all over it. Naturally there would be no danger to the Duck. The Admiral sensed the Duck's interest and enthusiasm for Spoke's success.

"Both of you come down to my cabin at 1330 and I'll have the rest of the information for you. LT, you'll be reporting to CDR Forner from here on out. Make sure if you have any needs or questions, you contact him." Duck all but popped every button on his shirt. Already Spoke was getting nauseous.

That afternoon, he reported to the ADM's cabin. "Come in and be seated," the Admiral said in a generally congenial manner. He knew Marks did not drink, but he offered him a scotch anyway.

"No thanks, Admiral," Spoke replied.

The Duck was already there with his 20-year old single malt scotch half gone. Admiral Stewart sat, crossed his legs and began.

"Seems one of the Triads, the 14K, have been getting into heated disputes with the Teo-Chiew Triad over rights to distribute heroin in China and all over the Pacific Rim. It has now erupted into significant violence. Unfortunately, U.S. servicemen have been caught in the crossfire.

"INTERPOL has been investigating the relationship of heroin sales throughout the region. They have been compromised repeatedly by local law enforcement. Their request to SECDEF was for a Naval Intelligence Officer with field experience to be assigned to work with their task force. We are here. You are here. You now have a short leave of absence from SEAL Team and Vietnam. You'll have orders written for Hong Kong. This is not a cake walk and demands a steady hand on the stick."

The Admiral's aviation simile did not go unnoticed. Spoke's dad had used many during his growing up years.

"The question is how good are you? I called your Team Leader. He gave you extremely high marks for your field work, planning and savvy. He said of all the Intelligence Officers he'd worked with, you were the best he'd ever encountered and wanted to have you head back to BUDS and SEAL training."

Spoke's thoughts flashed to LCDR Randy Rogers. He was one cool cucumber under fire, and the two of them had bonded in a number of tight spots with only bad guys getting hurt when they easily could have had a disaster.

Spoke had stood up to the Military Assistance Command, Vietnam, (MACV) fools that constantly tried to have SEALS humiliated by doing assignments they weren't equipped or supported for. "Drawing fire" away from those idiots went a long way to endearing the SEALs to him.

"I hope you'll permit me to go back when this temporary assignment is over," Marks said.

"Believe me, it would be my honor to do just that. First, let's get you ashore and over to the INTERPOL office. Then we'll cross the other bridges later."

Marks sensed the meeting was over and since it was a foregone conclusion that he'd do it, he started to rise.

The Admiral quickly said, "Whoa, Big Fella. You don't even know what you're up against."

"Sir, would you deliberately try to torpedo me?"

"No, of course not."

" Then, with all due respect, I'm ready to do what I can to help our men."

"You're just like your old man. I'll have CDR Forner brief you on the boat ride in."

Thirty minutes later, Marks, with his sea bag, Forner and 37 other eager and anxious sailors crowded into the Mike boat. LCMs or "Mike" boats were the work horses of the Amphibious Navy. They hauled everything from men to engine parts from ship to ship or ship to shore. Slow and ungainly in the water, what they lacked in beauty, they more than made up in utility.

CHAPTER 16 – MEET FANG

Arriving at the quay wall, everyone scrambled up the gangway. Two blocks up into the Wan Chai District was the China Fleet Club, the best department store catering to western tastes in Hong Kong.

CDR Forner said he wanted to go in to buy a new camera lens for his Nikon F1. They had the best prices and would take American money without haggling. The China Fleet Club foyer also had a money exchange to trade US dollars to Hong Kong Won.

While Forner went up to the third floor, Spoke exchanged a couple of hundred US dollars into Hong Kong Won. Marks smiled to himself and waited. Like Japanese tourists in the U.S., American servicemen were easily marked by the size of their camera. The rich ones had big cameras and the lowly had small ones. There was also another size reference about Americans, but according to the street girls size didn't matter.

Leaving the China Fleet Club, they turned left and headed for Gloucester Street. Three blocks more was Hennessy Rd. Turning right, they went a block and turned into a rather non-descript stairwell.

Spoke noted that to the trained eye the stairwell was anything but non-descript. A wrought iron gate and one of those new protected CCTV cameras caught his eye immediately. CCTV was relatively new and the size of the fixture was hard not to notice, but Forner missed it completely. When they got to the door at the top of the stairs, Forner knocked. The door opened and a small Chinese man asked for ID. He then closed the door and disappeared. Three minutes later, another Chinese man motioned them in and returned their IDs.

Forner opened his mouth, but it was obvious he was new at this business and only a squeak came out. He feigned a coughing fit. Spoke took over and indicated that they were with the U.S. Navy's CTF 76 and had been asked to meet someone at this address. Forner was clearly a rank amateur at anything remotely resembling real field work in the intelligence world.

The second Chinese man gave a small polite bow and motioned them into a receiving area complete with a couch, several overstuffed chairs and a coffee table. He introduced himself as Hsu Feng Jyan. He smiled and said "Americans seem to remember me best as 'Fang'. I am an agent with INTERPOL."

Fang was a man of few words, but it was most noticeable that he spoke perfect English with an American accent. He explained he'd been raised and educated in the U.S. He'd grown up in Southern California and graduated from UCLA. He'd started out in Pre-Med, but ultimately ended up in Chemistry. He spoke English, Spanish, Mandarin and Cantonese fluently as well as passive abilities in Japanese, Korean, Thai and many of the dialects of Southeast Asia.

After a brief interlude where Forner shared a bit more than he needed to and Spoke shared a brief personal thumbnail biography, they got down to business.

Fang explained that their mission centered on a request from the CIA. Seems they were most interested in the drug trafficking coming out of the Golden Triangle and of the conflict with the Triads. The CIA's Air America airline was suffering due to crossfire issues and they wanted to get to the bottom of who was poisoning the drugs in Hong Kong. This had been bad for their business since the Teo-Chiew Triad had stopped all business with westerners until the 14KTriad was out of the picture. The 14K also blamed the Teo-Chiew. It was a circular war with no clear participants or winners.

Almost openly shocked, Spoke listened with growing doubt as to who and what he was doing working to help CIA drug operations continue. He was under the obvious disillusioned impression he was helping save U.S. servicemen's lives. What was he doing helping one Triad do away with another so the CIA could protect its drug assets in Laos and the Golden Triangle?

Fang sensed Spoke's uneasiness and said," Seems all the heroic bull-shit you signed up for may not be what is reality."

"You got that straight," retorted Spoke.

"Make no mistake Mr. Marks, you are helping save servicemen's lives. If you abandon this assignment, more of the HKR2 will be on the street killing sailors and other servicemen. Whatever is the ultimate goal of this drug war, we are only doing one small part, but our part is to wear the white hats. We're the good guys."

The Duck just sat stunned. He wasn't sure he'd heard Fang correctly and he was sure the Admiral didn't know what this was really all about. He looked at his watch and muttered a feeble excuse about heading back to the ship before dark with his newly bought treasure and headed for the door.

Fang waved a hand to the other INTERPOL agent to let him go. Spoke stayed seated.

"Remember, Commander, this data is strictly Secret," Fang said to the fast departing man. The Duck stumbled out, wide-eyed and obviously nervous.

Fang turned back to Spoke.

"Thank you, Lieutenant Marks. While you may not understand right now, our mission is great. Make no mistake. After the Admiral called this morning with your bio information, I was sure we had an honest and wise agent."

"Let's get one thing straight. I do not condone drugs or drug use or anything related – legal or otherwise. As far as I am concerned the CIA can go blow this out their asses. I'm here to help U.S. sailors keep from getting killed.

"Incidentally, they call me Spoke. I'll feel better about calling you Fang." He toned down realizing he was almost shouting.

"Fair enough. Again, most appreciated. Your Admiral said you would be idealistic only to a point. I am glad you and I share the same point of view. What is the significance of Spoke?"

"Long story short, my four-year-old son heard someone from the command call me a "Spook." He couldn't pronounce it clearly and called me a Spoke in front of CINCPACFLT. It stuck. Now, where do I bunk and work?"

"You will stay at the Hong Kong Hilton, and your work desk is over there in the corner. I will not introduce my other two partners as I do not want you to have too much information if there should ever be an unfortunate accident. I believe you understand."

Spoke smiled and nodded. "Well, let's get started."

"Oh, and one thing more, the Hong Kong Police take a very strict, dim view about anyone without a badge carrying a handgun. No guns. That being said, I will not frisk you every time we go out, but I have done as I was instructed to do and ankle holsters inside socks frequently get overlooked."

Fang smiled a cryptic smile and winked at Spoke.

CHAPTER 17 – MEET MEI-LI

The Hong Kong Hilton was like any other Hilton around the world except the rooms were smaller. The single queen-size bed reminded Spoke of home. The nagging urge to call and talk with his children was waging war with his common sense. He reminded himself he was back on an op and could not break radio silence. He spread his meager sea bag out into the closet and various drawers in the room. He was to meet Fang for dinner and then out on the street for a night in the Wan Chai.

Dinner was good, but did not rate the 5-stars the slick colored brochure claimed. Spoke noticed Fang did not drink anything but tea. He did not smoke and Spoke felt a kind of kindred spirit to him.

Since Spoke had received the Port Brief that explained how things were purchased, eaten and drunk in Hong Kong, he felt he knew better what to expect.

The water from known sources in the hotels was safe as was the sealed bottled water, however the girls needed to have a blue card. The closer the date of the government stamp to the current date, the less the chance a participant might bring home some uninvited guest.

Drunkenness or drugs were not tolerated in any form. Uniforms were strictly forbidden except for Shore Patrol due to the long reach of civil unrest from the U.S. press. Clean sports attire was the required 'uniform of the day.'

Spoke chose a newly purchased IZOD golf shirt and a Members Only jacket along with polyester sports slacks. Virtually identical to every other sailor on liberty, he'd fit right in.

Fang briefed him in a low voice after dinner. "When we leave here, we will go back to the office. We will walk like any other sailors on liberty down into the Wan Chai. While not your first rodeo, I'm sure it will be an eye opener to you."

Unlike daylight hours, the Wan Chai was a totally different place. Spoke was amazed at the life, loud music and lights that seemed to blossom from every door, alley and street. The music came from live bands as well as recordings. Smells of fried foods, stale liquor, smoke and exhaust filled the air. The wet sidewalks reflected the lights. Cars passed slowly. Pimps were hustling sailors to come see their stables. Madams were offering special deals to sailors looking for a good time, especially ones with big bankrolls.

An older madam pushed over to them, "You want good time? Free drinks. Best girls in Hong Kong. Clean. I give you virgin. Clean. Just checked by doctor. You come in now." Fang smiled and declined but motioned to Spoke that if he wanted a virgin, here was a good place. Spoke just shook his head.

Fang went on, "When they see cops, even undercover cops, they want you to have all the free entertainment and drinks you want so you will stay there. Keeps the fights and trouble to a minimum. Believe me, they spot us every time."

They moved back into the crowds and continued down the street. Fang turned into one club, the Jade Pagoda, and both of them were immediately surrounded by no less than 20 young girls wanting to offer drinks and more enjoyable pastimes if the two of them were men enough to prove their appreciation.

Suddenly, as if on a silent cue, the ladies all parted and an older, very beautiful woman stepped forward. She looked at Fang and Spoke and motioned ever so subtly to follow her. Not one word spoken. Every communication was with her eyes. She moved as though on ball bearings and as fluid as mercury. In the dim, smoky light, she looked about 25 and without a doubt had every move and motion calculated to thrill the very center of manhood thrown at her feet.

Through a beaded portal, she turned and smiled. In the dim light of a hanging, shaded light bulb, Spoke could see she wasn't a young lady by his standards, but without doubt, she was one of the most beautiful women he'd ever seen. Her genes were obviously oriental and Euro and took the best from all worlds. Fang smiled.

She closed and locked the fixed door to a small but well-organized office. She reached down and lifted the telephone receiver off the cradle. It was obvious she did not want to be disturbed. She then reached over and turned on some music to provide "white noise."

"Just in case," she purred quietly.

Fang moved closer and motioned for Spoke to move closer too. She dripped femininity. She smelled like jasmine, Spoke's favorite smell. She wasn't dripping in it like the other girls, just amazingly subtle.

In a voice barely above a whisper, she said several 14K men came in earlier that evening. Two of the pimps at the bar went out with the 14K men. They returned several minutes later and gathered their chicks with fierce looks and warnings that they were to score and score as much as they could. Most important, however, they were to score with "horse;" and not just any horse – Hong Kong Rock Two. They were to blame it on the Teo-Chiew any way they could; get caught, give markers, anything.

Gao Mei-Li had been in the entertainment business since she was 11. Her mother was a high-end Hong Kong hooker and her father was a staff member of the French Consulate. A detail he'd forgotten to mention was that his wife lived just outside of Paris and so when he returned to Paris, he had abandoned Mei-Li, a younger sister, Lian-Na, and her mom.

Mei-Li found herself on the street after her mother died in 1961, murdered by a Triad chief who was trafficking in young girls. She'd barely escaped being caught which meant being forced into a life outside of Hong Kong, a life of cruel prostitution and fraught with disease.

Lian-Na had not been so fortunate. No one ever heard from her or about her again. Mei-Li hated the Triads and everything associated with them.

While INTERPOL provided a small stipend for her information, it was Fang that kept her in most essential things. True, the Jade Pagoda did alright, but the pimps and Triads took their shares leaving barely enough to restock and repair the place. Living expenses had to be obtained in more traditional ways.

Like her girls, she too had a blue card, but her clientele were very discreet members of upper society and the government who always used protection. To her, Fang, on the other hand, was true love. She admitted that he brought out a fierce emotion she'd only felt toward her mother and sister. She truly loved him deeply. She wanted to go away and leave this rat-race and curl up safely in his arms and be protected forever.

She said she would contact him immediately if the 14K men came back. They shared a gentle loving kiss and separated.

Back out on the street Fang was all business. Several more stops netted them nothing. As they turned to go up toward the office, a young Anglo caught their eye. He was acting very nervous and jumpy. First off, he was alone. Secondly, he was concealing a package very poorly. He turned and started away from them. They followed.

It was obvious he was new to the area and did not know where he was or where he was going. He looked again at them and ducked into an alley.

Thinking he could just slip away, he realized all too soon that the alley was a blind alley. The stench of the rotting garbage and stale alcohol indicated they were behind some restaurants or bars. Quickly he ran out of places to go and with extreme nervous excitement, he turned and produced a 9mm Smith and Wesson automatic.

As if on cue, Fang and Marks each moved away from each other to the alley walls. They looked like they'd practiced this procedure for years and sensed the other's moves.

As the two got closer to the very frightened man, he yelled he had a gun and he'd kill them if they didn't leave him alone. Nervously pointing at each back and forth, he was the image of absolute panic.

Fang quietly urged him to put the gun down. They didn't want to rob him or take his money. They just wanted to do business. Fang reasoned in his own mind that if the man had HKR2, he would be their first solid lead.

From his accent, they deduced he was an American. He continued to move his pistol back and forth.

Spoke feigned stumbling and went down to his knee. Drawing his small Beretta Minx, a 22 short "pocket gun," he came up and screamed an adrenaline powered yell that would have made rebels charging with Pickett at Gettysburg proud. It also would have shaken the bricks off buildings if any were loose.

"Get down on your face, now!" was the command. The noise of his "command voice" was so loud, Fang almost went down on his face.

Fang had his .357 Smith and Wesson revolver out of its holster and trained on the man. As though hit with a bolt of lightning, the youth hit the pavement, face down. Quickly, from under his coat, Fang raised his radio and called for back-up. Within minutes, Hong Kong Police were swarming all over the alley.

"He has a gun! He has a gun!" the young man kept pleading as he was taken away. He hoped that such a revelation would mitigate his own situation.

A local uniformed inspector looked at Spoke who just shrugged his shoulders and said he didn't know what the man meant. Fang then showed his fake Hong Kong Police badge and credentials. The crowd at the street end of the alley gradually dispersed, but eyes spotted Spoke and Fang – knowing eyes, eyes that would not forget a face.

Fang had been issued the fake credentials to protect his undercover status and liaison between INTERPOL and the Hong Kong Police. It helped in the past and apparently helped now. After a few more minutes, they left and walked toward the office.

CHAPTER 18 – MEI-LI'S HORROR

The next morning, the phone rang in Spoke's room at a cheery four in the morning. Seems sleep is a non-sacred tool regardless of the location or reason. He'd barely showered the day's dirt off and fallen into bed when Fang's voice rousted him.

"Just got a call. Get to the office, now!" The message was terse, simple and unemotional.

Upon climbing the stair at the Interpol office and clearing his credentials at the door, Spoke found a very somber Fang and two other officers he presumed to be Interpol agents standing around a table. No one spoke but it was obvious there was definitely something wrong.

"Mei-Li is in the hospital. A half hour after we left, some goons from the 14K Triad came in and beat her up bad enough they thought she was dead. Seems someone, probably one of the pimps, thought we were the police. Don't know how, but we now have to modify our approach. "

"The only people who saw us do anything remotely similar to police action were in that alley with that American," replied Spoke.

"I know. That's what worries me. If anyone in any of the bars reported us as anything other than police or Shore Patrol, we are in serious trouble."

Shore Patrol or undercover Hong Kong police frequently entered the Wan Chai bars to check the girls for Blue Cards and to make sure peace was being kept. Normally this was a regular occurrence and everyone was friendly and appreciated the cops being there. It kept fights to a minimum and made sure no one was doing illegal drugs on their premises. In general, it kept the doors open and their establishments on the "open and welcome list" for the military Port Briefing.

Almost always, the Madams knew who the police were and made sure they were kept very happy. This time someone knew Fang and Spoke were not. They also knew Mei-Li was very friendly with Fang. The real question was how much did she tell them and what did the 14K or any of the Triads for that matter know about them or their operation. Who was on the inside and on the Triad payroll?

Fang and Spoke left the office reporting to the others there that they would be on their car radio if anything changed with Mei-Li. They also said they were going directly to the Jade Pagoda and then the hospital.

The first stop instead was the Queen Elizabeth Hospital. Mei-Li was in room 212. It was a private room on the second deck, heavily guarded and secured by Hong Kong Police and the British Constabulary. Additional vetting was done by two plain clothes agents of an unknown police agency, but still very recognizable as policemen.

Windows were shuttered and heavily draped. This room had the tightest security Spoke had ever seen in a hospital. Doctors were vetted by the British and clearly every pill and injection checked and double-checked by everyone.

Mei-Li looked like a copy of the mummy. She had tubes and bandages everywhere. If she hadn't been identified previously, there was no way she could be identified now. Fang walked over to the closet. He quietly and almost imperceptibly motioned Spoke to join him.

Sure enough, the faint odor of jasmine met both of their noses in spite of the sterile smells of the room. Her clothes were covered with blood and were torn, clearly showing she had been roughed up pretty badly.

To her credit, the one place her exposed skin showed signs of a struggle were her fingernails. The three that could be seen clearly were split and had blood on them. Good for her, thought Spoke. I hope that was an eye she got.

Fang walked over to the doctor.

"When do you think we can talk to her?"

"It is hard to say. She is hurt very bad. We have her heavily sedated and will until we can get her vitals improved," the doctor quietly admitted. "We weren't sure we'd be able to save her. We almost lost her several times. She's a strong person with a strong will to live."

Fang wanted to tell him that not only did she want to live for herself, but she wanted to live for her sister and to find her.

Fang asked the on-duty police officers who the cops were that were first on the scene. Getting their names, he and Spoke left and headed for their precinct office. A quick visit with the dispatcher's log showed an on-scene response time of two minutes from the first call – that had to be a world's record! Unless......

Neither Fang nor Spoke believed in coincidences. If the two cops that responded that fast knew Mei-Li was not dead, the Triads knew too. Was it specifically the 14K or who? The 14K had been in the bar the night before. Threats to the girls from their pimps were from the 14K messengers. Everything spelled 14K. It was just too neat.

They had to get to those cops. Until she woke up and could tell them, they would not know who did what to her. They had to protect Mei-Li.

Fang pulled Spoke aside. "How serious is your Navy about getting these drugs out of Hong Kong?"

"I was told to pull out the stops," was the reply.

"I'm going to let you prove it," said Fang.

CHAPTER 19 – THE NAVY GETS INVOLVED

"Office of the Commander in Chief, Pacific, this is an unsecured line." The voice was hollow and sounded a long way off.

"Senior Chief Ramsey? Is that you?" Spoke chuckled as he spoke. He'd always been able to recognize voices even from questionable sources. There were "tells" that indicated stresses and idiosyncrasies in every voice. Even disguised voices had them. Just be patient and they surfaced, Spoke would always say.

"Spoke! I thought you died!" followed by a belly laugh.

"No and you still owe me for that night I bailed you out in San Diego! (More laughter).

"Alright Senior, I didn't call to haunt you for your first-born, but I do need to talk to the boss."

"Sir, you just missed him. He'll be back in about two hours unless it's an emergency."

"Senior, it is an emergency and it is about as important as the nuclear launch codes. It's really critical and a lot of lives are riding on this one. Ask him go to over to Intel as soon as possible. Have him call the SCIF at our Hong Kong Embassy. I'll be there in 15 minutes and will wait for his call."

"Roger that. And as far as my first born, you can have him, no strings attached."

"Let me ask the wife." Spoke smiled. The phone went dead.

American Embassy, Hong Kong

Spoke and Fang raced to the embassy entrance. Two Marines blocked their vehicle. "Gentlemen, this entrance is closed."

"Corporal, we are here on a mission of National Security and CINCPACFLT is calling in five minutes," Spoke barked with the authority that would have melted the golden stripes off his sleeves. Handing him his identification card, he demanded who was with the Ambassador this evening.

"Sir, Admiral Stewart is there with other dignitaries," was the crisp reply.

"Perfect! Is CDR Forner there also?"

"Yes, Sir!"

"Interrupt CDR Forner with a call IMMEDIATELY and tell him it is an emergency of National Security at the gate and that I am being detained here! NOW!!"

"Yes, Sir!"

Two minutes of silence followed by the Corporal bracing to the telephone and quickly placing the receiver back on the cradle which led to a startled Private First Class being told to escort the two gentlemen to the side door of the embassy building. There, standing inside were three very formally attired and very dignified gentlemen with extremely grave looks on their faces, U.S. Ambassador George Starke, RADM Stewart, and CDR Forner.

Dismissing the still very startled PFC, the Admiral looked at Marks and motioned to CDR Forner, "At least you went through the right channels to report to me."

"All right, LT, so much for the dramatics, what is the National Security issue?"

"Sir, this is Hsu Feng Jyan — Fang for short. He's our INTERPOL liaison. Mr. Ambassador, I'm LT Kevin Marks, the Navy's liaison agent on this operation. I am expecting a call from CINCPACFLT, Admiral Donophan, any moment now regarding transferring a Hong Kong national and key witness against the Triads and Hong Kong Rock 2 who was badly beaten this morning. They thought she was dead, but is under heavy security guard at Queen Elizabeth Hospital. She was found by two policemen in record time this morning – something that stinks about being in the right place at the wrong time by the wrong people. Blue Ridge is in the harbor. We could transport her there with the right permissions and be treated aboard. The call is for you, Admiral, but since you, both ambassadors and the ship are here, you can take care of business with no middle man."

"Breathe, LT, breathe. I'm impressed. You did that in two breaths. I did say SECDEF was pressing me, did I not? Mr. Ambassador, could you intercede with Ambassador Lieu? We would appreciate expediting the transfer of Miss, uh, Miss.... "

"Miss Gao, Gao Mei-Li," responded Fang.

"Miss Gao," the Admiral repeated.

"Immediately," responded Ambassador Starke. The Ambassador turned to a man in a tux and motioned for him to take the group to the SCIF.

The CIA Station Chief led the group up to the SCIF on the second floor. The SCIF was where all classified communication occurred and was a small room with an ante room protected by a heavy vault door and combination lock. The one-way mirrored window obviously had someone behind it because the inner door buzzed when the small group entered. The Admiral and CIA man continued to the inner room, but no one else was permitted inside. Time passed. Fifteen minutes later the Admiral came out with his poker face on.

"Seems SECDEF and SECNAV have been on CINCPAC's ass as well. Let's get her out to Blue Ridge. I'll contact CAPT Bowen to get to flight quarters. You're sure she's that important?"

"Sir, I guarantee it," responded Spoke. "Do we have access to a Medevac chopper here?"

"LT, this is a hell of a time to think of that!" the Admiral fumed. "As this operation is going to have to be concealed, it will have to be at night and no doubt be a covert action. Damn! What I wouldn't give for a bird farm right now!" A "bird farm," of course, was an aircraft carrier.

The knock was low, but subtle. The CIA man went to the door and cracked it open. Standing in the passage way were two men; one American and one Chinese, both in tuxedoes.

"Gentlemen, could you please step out into the hall?" was the request by the American. Ambassador Starke presented Ambassador Lieu to each of the men.

"Ambassador Lieu has given permission for the transfer to your ship with one very big condition; you must not leave Hong Kong territorial waters."

"Mr. Ambassador, that suits us fine," replied Admiral Stewart. In his mind, however, he was thinking that if CINCPAC was directed by SECNAV, SECDEF and the President, Department of State will have to figure that forgiveness and permission are two greatly divergent issues.

"We do have a serious problem, Mr. Ambassador. This has hit so suddenly that we have no transportation available and this will have to be done at night; preferably tonight."

"Admiral, Mr. Ambassador, Gentlemen. You are all sacrificing so much for we of Hong Kong. What would we be if we could not help ourselves? Please leave the transport issue to me. We will be at Queen Elizabeth Hospital helipad in two hours. Please have her ready to be transported."

CHAPTER 20 - TRAGEDY

Queen Elizabeth Hospital, Hong Kong

Draped and covered, the gurney with the mummy rolled out of room 212 surrounded by an armed escort of eight men and three doctors as well as two nurses. There was hardly room enough for movement much less anything else. Fang and Spoke watched with interest and concern. They held the doors to the elevator. The elevator groaned under the weight of the group. They only had to go up two floors and then out to the helipad where the modified British-marked medevac UH-1 waited, its rotors turning.

Fang started to get in but the pilot motioned a cut-off signal signifying that there were too many on board already. He'd have to find another way out to the ship. He and Spoke looked at each other and ran to the shelter of the hospital. It had already started to drizzle again; that stinking, constant cold drizzle. It also would mean the medevac would have to fly under the ceiling with lights on, not something generally done except in an emergency. This was such an emergency.

A quick call on the telephone to the duty desk at the Shore Patrol Office resulted in an obviously busy Petty Officer who yelled over the din at his end of the call to wait a second. The order to hold the midnight liberty launch fell on deaf ears. Too many drunks had priority. In between yells to shut up, and as nicely as he could, the Petty Officer of the Watch informed this unknown voice that perhaps he could persuade the Admiral to make room on his barge for a ride back.

Dialing the Embassy telephone number, the switchboard operator confirmed that the Admiral's party was just getting ready to leave. Spoke all but begged to talk to CDR Forner. He gritted his teeth, but sucked up his pride. "CDR Forner, LT Marks. We couldn't get on the chopper going to the Blue Ridge. Can we get on the Admiral's Barge with your party?"

"I'll check with the boss," was the answer. After a moment the reply, "He said be at the landing in 15 or you swim." Spoke was sure the last part of swimming was Forner's addition. It was apparent that Forner was in his height and glory, the little jerk.

Fang and Spoke raced from the hospital driving through Hong Kong breaking virtually every known traffic law in the book. Spoke had a firm grip on reality, but this was insane.

Fang was not going to miss that boat. Just as they screeched to a halt at the head of the quay wall, they saw the Admiral's car arriving. The Admiral also saw Spoke and Fang. He motioned for them to park in the vacant stall left for dignitaries next to his vehicle. They got out of their respective vehicles.

"She obviously made the medevac," the Admiral stated. "We owe the Hong Kong Ambassador a letter of appreciation for that one. CDR could you please take that for action?" Spoke smiled inwardly on that one. The little weasel would have to do something besides strut around figuratively wearing the Admiral's stars.

Turning back to the harbor, the myriad of boats and lights were almost hypnotizing to Spoke. One light blossomed brightly and caught everyone's eye. It looked like an upside down comet. Suddenly a brilliant light erupted in the sky. Reflexively, Spoke closed his eyes. The USS Blue Ridge was highlighted as burning debris arched away from the explosion into the black water below.

On the quay wall, sailors were stunned. The sound finally reached the shoreline. Several thought the Blue Ridge was hit and started to lose emotional control. Others recognized that it occurred between the ship and shore. They were trying to calm their shipmates. Local girls who'd accompanied the sailors to the quay wall for one last attempt at "true love" were crying and screaming.

The Admiral was already on the radio and attempting to contact his Duty Officer on Blue Ridge.

"What the hell happened, Jim!" he yelled.

"Sir, it appears the helo failed to identify properly and was being held off until they could make sure it was the right flight. Blue Ridge sick bay was standing by and our Marine contingent was ready to escort and guard the package. It appears an unidentified and blacked out "bum boat" launched a SAM. No casualties on Blue Ridge. They've dropped two small boats with swimmers and medics looking for survivors from the helo. Over."

"Roger. Keep me posted. I'll be standing by. Out." The Admiral fumed. "Who the hell knew we were sending anything out to the ship? Marks!!"

"Sir!"

"Did you or your sidekick say anything or do anything to let this cat out of the bag?" While keeping it a very low volume, the intensity of the question said volumes.

"No, Sir. In fact, our entire op was based solely on the success of this movement and the good health of that person. Sir, Fang and Mei-Li were in love. He would never have jeopardized her or the op either. We tried ourselves to get on the bird."

Spoke looked at Fang. In the short two days he'd known Fang, he felt he'd known him all his life. They were kindred spirits. They thought alike. They felt alike and they surely would never have allowed this to willingly happen.

Fang looked like he was in shock. Spoke had closely observed his new partner. He'd never seen emotion even so much as surface the least bit, except when he looked at Mei-Li. In the lights of Hong Kong, he could see the tears in his eyes. Yes, he and Fang were two of a kind; the kind you wanted at your back and not mad at you.

"I take it you don't want a ride back to the ship now, Mr. Marks," queried the Admiral softly.

"No, Sir. Thanks, I think we'll be burning the midnight oil for a while," replied Spoke. He walked over to Fang and guided him towards his car.

"Want me to drive?" Spoke asked quietly.

"No." was the equally quiet reply.

Again, in the crowd a set of eyes watched impassively and with no emotion.

CHAPTER 21 – WHAT NOW?

0230 28 Feb 1972 Hong Kong Hilton Hotel, Hong Kong

The urge to go back to INTERPOL Headquarters was almost overwhelming. Room service brought up a roll-away cot and some toiletries. Fang used the bathroom and collapsed on the bed.

Spoke took the cot. He knew it had been at least 58 hours since Fang had seen a bed and that would greatly impair his judgment as well as his stamina. Spoke already felt the effects of sleep deprivation and felt he was smart enough to do the right thing having Fang here with him.

He placed the cot in the entry way of the room to block passage to the hall in or out. Since the only ones that knew he was there were the ones at INTERPOL Headquarters, he'd discreetly placed a call to the duty officer to wake them only in the event of a real emergency.

He also told the hotel concierge that they were not to be disturbed for anything short of a fire. Both he and Fang needed at least 8 hours of undisturbed shut-eye.

Early the next morning, a sharp rap at the door sent both occupants vertical immediately. Each looked at the other questioningly. "Who is it?" barked Spoke.

"Lee," came the terse reply.

Agent Lee was one of the INTERPOL operatives. Since both men were already dressed, they moved the cot and permitted the INTERPOL agent in.

"You were right, you were being watched last night again," Lee stated in a whisper. Fang listened carefully and was now fully awake.

"Was it who we thought?" he asked.

"Yes. And he was so intent on you that he led me back to their head-quarters as well. 14K has competition and a very interesting payroll."

"Well….?" Spoke started.

"Not here!" Lee and Fang both said almost simultaneously, quietly intense motioning around the room with their fingers and cupping their hands to their ears. Spoke got the message.

Spoke, Fang and Lee quickly headed back to INTERPOL Headquarters. Inside, five men worked feverishly at a table with a map and several detailed lists. Several others were manning several telephones. Six of the men were especially vetted and on loan from the Hong Kong Police. The others were Fang's Interpol agents.

The lists were in Chinese but the map had several annotations that gave Spoke a quick idea what was happening. He waited patiently for Fang to finish the meeting.

"Wanna share?" Spoke asked quietly.

"Soon was going to get lunch at Sun-Sing, and Lee was to get dessert at Ya-Lo. We all meet back here at 1200."

Fang's attempt at humor was noted, but since it had been almost two days since Spoke had eaten he was really not in the mood.

"Let's go get something to eat," said Spoke with an appeal in his voice.

Fang nodded and they left and headed to Fang's car.

"And what does your inner self need as comfort food?" smiled Fang. "I know of a great Vietnamese restaurant over by the tram to Victoria Peak."

"Vietnamese!? In the garden spot of the greatest Chinese cuisine in the modern world. You want to eat Vietnamese?!" Spoke stifled a laugh that would have caused Fang to drive off the road except for the concerns weighing on his mind.

"I just thought you'd be missing it by now," responded Fang laughing. Seems a little bit of sleep really turns him into a funny guy. Note to self, keep him away from the pillow.

The drive to the restaurant took less time than he expected. Spoke watched the people going about their lives totally oblivious to the life and death struggles occurring in the seedier parts of their beautiful, albeit crowded, kingdom.

Fang had recovered a bit from the dreadful shock of the previous night's events, but still drifted into a silent stare that worried Spoke. He'd seen it before after operations in Vietnam with young SEALS who'd seen buddies get severely wounded or killed. He didn't know Fang well enough yet to know how quickly Fang would recover from the shock. He wasn't sure how long SECDEF would let him stay here either.

They arrived at Phoc Do, a garden spot of Vietnamese cuisine, and parked the car. The smells quickly met him at the door and transported him back to Saigon. Thoughts of his first visit to the small street-side restaurant and the beautiful, young waitress flooded his mind.

Quickly he forced them from his memory. A very nice woman led them to a table and offered them menus in English and Chinese. Wrapped chop sticks were already at their places resting on the napkins. She politely asked if they needed forks. Both shook their heads in the negative.

"You like drink?" she asked.

"Coca Cola and tea," Spoke motioned to himself and Fang. She nodded and headed back to the back.

"What's good?" Fang asked Spoke.

"Take a look around. If you see what someone else has and it looks and smells good, point and ask for that. If not, you're on your own," Spoke smiled remembering his first lesson in Vietnamese eating from Bee.

Most restaurants catered to tourists and had plastic mock-ups in windows with the numbers by the dishes clearly labeled. That didn't mean much if you didn't care for the spices, so it took a while before a person was comfortable eating different dishes. Plastic mock-ups only went so far.

"I'm going to have some Pho. Try it and see. Ma'am." Said Spoke. "Two Pho dinners." He signaled two fingers and she nodded.

Dinner proceeded normally and Spoke watched Fang casually, but intently. He was waiting for him to manifest signs of undo stress or continued issues of emotional instability. He needed to know the man on his six o'clock was going to be there for him when the going got rough. He also needed to know that he would not go to pieces.

Finished, Spoke paid the bill promising to let Fang get the next one. They got into Fang's Toyota. Instead of turning toward the city center, they turned away toward Victoria Peak. The road wound around and foliage lined the sides of the road. Fang pulled off into a driveway out of sight of the roadway.

"What's up? Where we goin'?" Spoke asked. Fang did not respond but watched the rear-view mirror intently.

A black Mercedes passed the semi-hidden driveway. Two men were in the car. The car was speeding up and the driver obviously was intent on trying to locate something he seemed to have lost.

Fang waited a few more seconds and pulled out turning left, the opposite direction from the Mercedes' travel. Increasing speed, he headed to the next intersecting road and turned right. He pulled off and turned off his engine. Again he waited.

In less than a minute, the Mercedes flew by. Slamming on its brakes, it almost went out of control. Out of sight for only a few seconds, Fang motioned for Spoke to slump down in his seat.

The Mercedes came back into view slowly. From his adjusted rear-view mirror, Fang could see the driver and passenger carefully scanning the seemingly parked and abandoned car. They were obviously following them for a reason. What did they know? Who were they? Fang had to find out.

The Mercedes occupants seemed very hesitant about coming near the Toyota. They clearly seemed worried about something. They pulled their car off the road.

Just under a half hour later, three vehicles passed. One was a marked Hong Kong police vehicle. The Mercedes decided it was time to move. Slowly it moved forward, out of their line of sight.

Thirty minutes later, Fang smiled and finally moved. Quietly, he muttered,

"Now it's our turn to be the cat."

"Mind telling me what that was all about?" Spoke asked.

"Watch and see, my friend, watch and see," smiled Fang in a determined almost evil way.

He pulled the car ahead slowly, crunching gravel quietly. Slowly he turned the Toyota around and eased it toward the corner. There it was. The tail of the black Mercedes appeared about 200 meters down the road pointed down the hill. Suddenly it came to life and started to execute an about face.

"Let's have some fun with you," smiled Fang as he turned away from the Mercedes. He picked up his radio microphone.

"Base, Unit Two," he said. Static followed by "Unit Two, go." "Unit Two has lice on Vic Peak Drive. Needs dip."

"Roger, Two, WILCO, out."

Within two minutes the cars that had previously gone up the hill came down the hill and U-turned behind the Mercedes. The marked Hong Kong police car also pulled up and turned on its police lights.

The Mercedes slowed down and finally pulled over. The marked police car pulled up ahead of the Mercedes. The other two black Toyotas then passed the Mercedes and proceeded up the hill. It was very obvious that the Mercedes driver was quite shook up.

The uniformed Hong Kong policeman approached the Mercedes. "You appear to be lost. Can I help you find where you are going?"

"No, officer. We were just looking for a lookout place to see the city. We're just tourists," the driver was clearly struggling to keep his emotional fear from the police officer.

"Well, go up two blocks and turn right. It'll lead you to the lookout parking lot," the officer smiled.

Down the road Fang slowed and watched the exchange.

"Amateurs," was all Fang could mutter.

Whoever these surveillance teams were, they were going to have to get better if they were going to play with the big boys. Surely they weren't 14K or Teo-Chiew or even the American CIA. Those boys were really good and definitely would not make the mistakes these Bozos were making.

The three Toyotas separated at the fork in the road and Fang pulled off at the second protected drive. The marked police car passed and the "escorted" Mercedes passed as well. After they were safely out of sight, Fang backed out of the drive and headed back toward the city. The ruse would keep the Mercedes occupied for hours.

Once back into the hustle and bustle of Hong Kong proper, Fang headed for Xao Lieu Mortuary. Parking down the street, they walked toward the entrance. Spoke knew that the oriental ways of honoring the dead were totally different than western ways and jumped to the conclusion that Fang had heard about bodies recovered from the explosion and helo wreck the night before.

They entered and were met with the strong, earthy, pungent smell of incense. Several mourners were huddled together consoling a very distraught woman. Fang walked toward a door opposite where they were standing.

A veiled woman stepped forward to block their way and then stepped back. No words were spoken. The door was opened, but no light revealed what was behind it. Quickly they entered. The door safely closed, the dark curtain was opened and a dimly lit room became visible. Several tables similar to autopsy tables surrounded by cabinets and lights that were turned off were seen as their eyes adjusted.

A thin white ray of light emanated under a door at the far end of the room against the polished tile. Even though it was less than a millimeter in width, it seemed like a beacon due to their eyes adjusting to the dark. Both moved toward it.

Fang tapped lightly on the door. "Enter," was the response in Chinese.

Fang opened the door to a flood of light. This seemed to blind both men momentarily. Fang looked on unemotionally, but Spoke's breath caught in his throat. It was a mummy with split fingernails. This had to be Mei-Li! But we saw her loaded on the chopper, Spoke thought. I saw it explode. She is supposed to be dead. Then who did we load and how did we play that one out? He looked ever so hard at Fang who continued to look at Mei-Li.

"How's she doing, doctor?" Fang asked in Chinese. "Has she regained any vitals?"

"I'm afraid not," he replied. "Time is a two-edged sword, young man. She has a strong will to live and very strong need to fulfill her destiny. It is also working in a way that may not help you get to the bottom of your investigation quickly, however."

"Thank you, doctor," replied Fang with a bow. "Again, your wisdom and kindness is appreciated." Turning to Spoke he stated flatly, "Let's go. I'll fill you in on the details."

CHAPTER 22 – MORE PIECES TO THE PUZZLE

Kowloon-Hong Kong Ferry Pier, Kowloon

The crouching uniformed Kowloon Prefecture Policeman looked up at Hong Kong Police inspector Xiu. The naked body he leaned over had not been in the water for more than a couple of hours. The Coroner arrived as they were talking. Other policemen had cordoned off the area and were keeping the gawking crowds back.

This was a bad time, a busy time at the ferry depot. Since Hong Kong never slept, thousands of people were returning from work in Hong Kong or headed to Hong Kong for the night life or work. Any way you looked at it, there were a lot of people at the depot.

"You know the drill, Officer," said Xiu.

"Yes, Sir," responded the policeman.

Xiu walked away and over to his car. Eyes watched from the crowd. Eyes that knew. Eyes that belonged to someone used to seeing death, all kinds of death.

Back at Interpol Headquarters the telephone rang. Soon picked it up, "Soon." He nodded to Fang. Fang motioned for Soon to put it on hold. Fang then picked it up. "Hsu." His face then went blank. His eyes definitely showed familiarity with the caller. "When? .... We'll be down immediately."

Both he and Spoke climbed into Fang's Toyota. Spoke looked at Fang. "Wanna share now?"

"Sorry, I've had my mind on some other things." He recovered. "It seems we have an unauthorized, swimsuit-optional bather at the ferry terminal in Kowloon. He obviously didn't read the signs saying he needed a bathing suit at that location. His body was taken to the city morgue here in Hong Kong. The Chief Inspector thought we might be able to recognize him since he was wearing only a smile. It might be one of our visitors from the Mercedes today."

It was not a long drive to the morgue. Actually, it was not a long drive anywhere in Hong Kong proper. It was just the crowds and traffic that made it seem longer than it really was. They pulled up and parked the car.

Both men walked through a rear door. The sterile smell of anti-septic assaulted their noses. The ceramic tile and stainless steel echoed their footsteps. Compared to the alternative of dead bodies, Spoke rationalized, the smells of the anti-septic was acceptable. He'd smelled enough dead things in Vietnam.

They turned to the left and saw the inspector standing by two men in white lab coats.

A body lay on a stainless table with many of the organs already removed. The ligature marks on the neck seemed very obviously the cause of death.

Regarding the body more closely, Fang and Spoke detected the extremely faint odor of almonds. They looked at each other; cyanide. Seems whoever wanted the swimmer dead, really wanted him dead. The identity was straight forward.

The Medical Examiner stated that yes, he smelled the odor and surmised the ligature marks on the neck were aimed at an amateur so that the real cause of death would be hidden. He then went on to explain that the neck marks had not bruised enough to warrant being the true cause of death.

"That was the driver that followed us this afternoon, Inspector," Fang stated flatly. "I did not get a clear look at the passenger, but without a doubt, this man was the driver. Do we have an I.D.?"

As an additional clue to identity, Fang and Spoke noticed the small tattoo on his forearm. The Medical Examiner had not mentioned it, but Fang knew immediately what it signified.

"Not yet. We are working on it. Thank you for coming down," said the inspector quietly.

Names were not used in the morgue for obvious reasons. No one at that location was vetted to know about INTERPOL's drug operations there in Hong Kong much less their current mission, not even the coroner.

Fang and Spoke turned and walked out of the building the same way they came in. Fang wanted desperately to return to see how Mei Li was, but instead headed for the Hilton. Dropping off Spoke he headed for his own place. It had been three days since he'd been there and he needed a shower and his own bed in a much needed way.

CHAPTER 23 – FINALLY, SOME ANSWERS

Spoke awoke with a start. Something inside startled him into consciousness. It wasn't something he heard, at least he thought. It seems he'd developed a sixth sense over the last seven months since his time in Vietnam. He heard something again that was almost imperceptible. Perhaps it was a mouse. Perhaps it was an insect. Perhaps it was nothing. Spoke started to relax.

It was early morning. The darkness yielded reluctantly to the very faint light of dawn. Cloudy gray light was peeking through the edges of the dark curtains of the room.

There it was again. This time he was sure it was something and something wrong.

Slowly the door opened and a dark form quietly slipped into the room. The door closed with a light snick as the latch caught the strike.

The stealthy, dark form quietly moved toward the bed. It started to reach down toward the occupant. Suddenly the lights went on. Spoke blocked the exit to the room holding his small pocket gun.

"Just what do you think you're doing?!" demanded Spoke.

"Relax, my friend," Fang laughed. "You're safe. I just wanted to see if you had the reflexes you seemed to have. You pass."

"Damn it, Fang!" forced Spoke. "You almost got shot."

"With that? That couldn't hurt a cockroach," laughed Fang.

"Well tell that to Abraham Lincoln. What were you thinking anyway?"

Motioning quickly with his hands cupped behind his ears, he said, "Shhhh. Lincoln was shot with a 44."

Fang then motioned with his finger to his lips and circled the room. He took a pad and pencil. Quickly he wrote: 'Went to office earlier. Swimmer member of the Chinese PLA. Small tattoo on arm marked him as one of theirs.'

What wasn't said was why strangle someone after cyanide unless it was to cover up why they had been murdered. But why the Chinese and why the People's Liberation Army in with the Triads?

"Get dressed. I'll wait in the coffee shop. And next time, keep your door locked." He laughed as he walked out.

"It was locked!" snapped Spoke laughingly raising his voice at the disappearing figure.

Spoke headed for the bathroom. He kept asking himself what the PLA was doing with the Triads in Hong Kong. Were they involved with the Triads over HKR2? Why was the CIA involved with the Triads? Was the CIA involved with the PLA too?

The thoughts kept going over in his mind as he took care of his necessities. Why would they kill their own people? So many questions. So few answers.

Finished, he dressed and headed for the coffee shop. He spotted Fang in a corner booth. He motioned to the maître-de that his party was waiting and headed for Fang's table. The smell of bacon, sausage and other American breakfast delights overwhelmed his hungry stomach which growled its urgent need for filling.

"What's good?" Spoke smilingly asked.

"Look around. When you see something you like, point at it and tell the waitress that you want some of that," replied Fang laughing. "Works every time."

"I'm ordering a good ol' American breakfast of link sausage, bacon, scrambled eggs and hash browns with whole wheat toast and orange juice." He looked at Fang. "What're you having?"

"All I wanted was some rice and hot tea," was the simple reply. "I can't understand what Americans see in their heavy breakfasts."

"Breakfasts are the most important meal of the day," jested Spoke. "You can go all day with little else when you start out firing on all cylinders."

Then in a quiet voice he said, "Tell me what you can here. My mind is going crazy with questions."

"Me too, but nothing here. It will have to wait until we get back to the office."

Time stood still while breakfast was prepared, served and eaten. Both men ate as quickly as they could without looking too conspicuous. Finished, Spoke signed the receipt billing the meal to his room and they both arose and headed for the door.

Once outside, the rain met them with the seemingly constant wet covering that enveloped the islands of Hong Kong. If it wasn't raining, it seemed to have a mist that hung like a heavy gray blanket over everything. Fang's car moved toward the Interpol office and parked in its usual location. They climbed the stairs and entered.

Almost bursting with questions, Spoke started quickly. "Why the PLA? What is the CIA doing with the commies? Is it over HKR2 or something else? What the hell is going on? What are the Triads doing?"

"Easy does it. Easy does it," Fang responded. Everyone in the room started laughing. "If this wasn't so serious, you'd be comical!"

"First of all, how is Mei-Li?" Spoke asked.

"As of this morning, she is both stable and improving. She's still unconscious, but the doctor feels she is strong and will be ready to talk to us in a few days," Fang said quietly. "We must still keep away from her for a few more days and permit the right time to question her to the doctor."

"Alright, what about the PLA driver? Do we know anything about him?" queried Spoke.

"That's where we need your help. Can you query your sources in Hawaii? We can't use the Ambassador's SCIF. CIA's too close on that one. Can you get out to the SCIF on the ship?"

"I'll leave right away. I also need to find out how long they will be here in Hong Kong. I'm afraid it won't be long. Normally, liberty ports are only three to five days. I guess it also depends on how many of the staff catch the 'screamin' heebee jeebies.' The other problem is that there was an incident of international proportions that could motivate her to sail," Spoke smiled at his own attempt at humor.

Fang motioned for Spoke to sit down and draft a request to the Admiral for his clearance to be passed to Blue Ridge.

"How long will this take?" asked Fang.

"Since this is going straight to the Admiral, it should be within the hour I would think," responded Spoke.

"We'll head down to the Shore Patrol office and hopefully have our answer by the time we get there. I don't know where the Admiral is right now, but if he is anywhere they can reach him, it will be quick."

The message sent, both intelligence officers then continued with their strategies and planning. As usual, they were assisted by the other two additional Interpol agents.

Their plans finished, they headed down to the landing and the Shore Patrol Office. Spoke walked in.

"Don't you guys ever sleep?" the First Class Petty Officer asked.

Spoke responded, "If the bad guys would give us a break, we'd love to. Besides, I'd like to get some new suits and shoes. Know anywhere good?"

"Chief said there was a great place over on Hennessey Road. I'll ask him for you, LT, but I bet you really want this," and handed him the message from Blue Ridge.

"Yes, and yes," responded Spoke motioning for Fang to join him. "When's the next launch?"

"Next one's at 1300. You've got time for lunch I expect." The Petty Officer nodded over his shoulder. "Bet your friend knows some great spots."

Both intelligence officers smiled, turned and walked toward Fang's car. "I think he was fishing for an invitation."

Fang smiled. "Believe me, he gets far better 'invites' for extracurricular activities, drinks and meals with that SP brassard on his arm than we ever would. Let's go over to the China Fleet Club. I don't want to miss that launch."

CHAPTER 24 – BLUE RIDGE

1330, 29 Feb 1972, Hong Kong Harbor, Hong Kong

The boat ride was fairly uneventful, except that Fang started to look a little green by the end of it. The wind chop on the harbor was not the easiest thing to endure in a Mike boat without a view of the horizon thanks to the high metal sides of the boat. The following wind drove the diesel fumes into the boat and the smell of the occasional drunk Sailor or Marine that left his lunch on the raised wood slats of the deck didn't help either.

Blue Ridge was anchored by the bow so she could swing with the wind. She had an accommodation ladder rigged from her starboard sponson deck, a large growth-like appendage running down 2/3 of her port and starboard sides and rising to her flat main deck. She bristled with antennas and radars. She was a large ship built on the same hull as the Iwo Jima class helicopter carriers. Dubbed a "McNamara Blunder," for her inability to stay afloat much less be anywhere on time and under budget was fairly well deserved.

Blue Ridge and Mt. McKinley, her sister ship on the East Coast, had the reputation for being "welded to the pier" due to constant repairs. She appeared top-heavy and for having only one screw and rudder, was notorious for breaking down at the most critical times even at sea and underway. This too was another of the "blunders" attributed to Blue Ridge and Secretary of Defense McNamara.

All that said, she was literally a floating hotel. Her 600+ ship's company could support up to 1200 embarked staff Marines or Army personnel. She had a complete Intelligence Center with several SCIFs. She had a fully functioning briefing studios with closed circuit TV, Flag bridge and living quarters as well as operations center. Her fully functional dental and medical center had several operating rooms. She had a Communication Suite with satellite up and down links and the most sophisticated listening abilities afloat.

The embarked staff officers loved her because they had their own staterooms complete with "valets" also known as Navy stewards. The ship's company officers had their own private mess. The enlisted ate like kings. The embarked staff officers also had their own mess. Of course when they first put out to sea, the motion of the ship usually negated the delicious meals sending many of the embarked Marine or Army personnel to stand around the garbage chute resembling the dipping bird toys that kids put around a glass of water. Ship's company always felt it was payback for the less than kind way some of the staff treated many of them. The best meals were always served the first day or so just to tease the embarked staff members who formed the contingent around the garbage chute.

The liberty launch finally moored itself loosely to the lowered platform. Fang almost kissed the Boatswain Mate as he passed him and staggered up the ladder. On the ceremonial Quarter Deck, the Chief of the Watch (called the Officer of the Deck) and Quartermaster stood in their whites and rain gear next to a self-important officer in khakis and his khaki "Ike" jacket.

The rain began again along with the wind. While LT Marks demonstrated proper Navy protocol and background by facing the stern of the ship where the colors were flying and coming to a quick attention, then facing the Chief of the Watch, he requested permission to come aboard. Acknowledged by the Chief, he showed his identification card. Fang just showed his ID. The officer in khakis stepped forward.

"Mr. Hsu, welcome aboard," CDR Forner looked condescendingly sideways at LT Marks. "Mr. Marks." Spoke nodded his head. The CDR went on, "The Admiral is in his Briefing Theater. I'll escort you up there. Petty Officer, please issue Mr. Hsu and LT Marks **escorted** visitor badges." The Quartermaster of the Watch complied and the men stepped inside the dry, well-polished tiled passageway. "Follow me, gentlemen."

Turning right, they went forward to the ladder and up to the second deck. Slightly forward of the ladder well, they turned outboard and faced a plain gray door with the four alpha/numeric code stenciled above it. The only thing outstanding about the door was the Marine sentry standing in front of it. Knocking brought a reply of "Enter." Rear Admiral Stewart stood from his chair and welcomed Mr. Hsu and LT Marks.

The room was arranged with an eight-foot table covered with a blue felt table cloth trimmed in dark yellow-gold and six large blue and dark yellow-covered chairs around it. In the center of the table was a device resembling a multi-line office telephone complete with an internal speaker. A key with plastic head was inserted into the face just to the right of the center. Marks knew the tan-colored phone was like the special encripted phones at CINCPACFLT in the Intelligence Center, the STU-III. These phones were totally secure and used to discuss all manner of classified subjects.

Admiral Stewart introduced his Chief of Staff, CAPT Dick Mortensen, and the Blue Ridge Captain, CAPT Robert Bowen. He invited Mr. Hsu and LT Marks to sit at the table while CDR Forner sat in a chair outside the circle. This caused Forner to do the slow burn. Remembering the look and treatment at the quarterdeck, Marks withheld his smile but felt like high-fiving everyone in the room.

Admiral Stewart started after everyone was seated. "LT, you called me. What do we need from ADM Donophan? I certainly hope it isn't a BBQ rib order from Fui's in Honolulu." Laughter was short and definitely stiff.

Spoke started, "Sir, we feel we have a serious breach in the security of the entire program. We have definite proof that the Triads are being pitted against one another by an outside source. Indicators point that the source, we feel, is either the CIA or China. Ms. Gao could have told us conclusively who beat her up. We feel it was one of those two entities who wanted her dead as opposed to the Triads.

"Yesterday, we were followed by a car. We were able to identify the driver when his very dead, stripped body turned up in Kowloon. He had tattoos identifying him as PLA. He and his partner used very sloppy techniques while shadowing us. This indicates that either China is new to this game and is trying to cover their trail, or CIA is trying to play them for fools. Either way, we need more horsepower than we have at this point to find out what is going on."

Fang watched closely for any signs or "tells" in anyone there, specifically the Admiral or CDR Forner. These men were really in the dark or they were a lot better at this game than he gave them credit for. He would have hesitated to play poker with them.

Spoke also watched intently. The one that really looked stupid was supposed to look that way and he came through loud and clear. Forner couldn't bluff if his life depended on it. Perhaps a poker game with him would be alright, thought Spoke.

"So our call to CINCPACFLT is to get him to go to SECNAV who in turn goes to SECDEF who goes to the President to order the CIA to divulge their operation here in Hong Kong and Southeast Asia. And we explain this when we tell him we have a dead PLA operative and a dead hooker and a hunch?" the Admiral summarized this with little to no emotion, but there was the slight bit of sarcasm in his voice. It appeared he wanted a stronger case if he was to lay his stars on the line.

"Sir, you told me this operation was to be a top priority and that it was to be done at all costs. It has already cost sailors, airmen, soldiers, Marines and others their lives. How much is one of those lives worth if they were your son or daughter?" Marks fired back, albeit without emotion and very evenly. He knew he'd hit below the belt on this one. The Admiral had lost a son to drugs while he was away on deployment. Marks also knew that it was one of the primary reasons the Admiral had not received the carrier group command he so dearly wanted. Instead he'd been stuck with the "Gators" to work out his penance. Here he had a perfect chance to do just that.

"Chief of Staff, place the call to CINCPACFLT."

"Aye, Sir."

CHAPTER 25 – NOW, THE REST OF THE STORY

The telephone call complete, the Admiral looked at each of the men in the room.

"Gentlemen, this does not get discussed outside of this room or with anyone else."

He looked straight at CDR Forner who squirmed uncomfortably in his chair. He excused the remainder of the room except Fang and Spoke. The door closed.

Thinking the two intelligence officers were going to get chewed out, CDR Forner almost skipped out of the room.

"What happened two nights ago?" the Admiral started. "And don't try blowing smoke up my skirt. I've played this game a lot longer than both of you combined." He was all business.

Fang cleared his throat. "Admiral, LT Marks knew nothing of this. I engineered it to expose who was working for the Triads and Chinese at the Embassy levels. Only me and her doctor knew the true condition of Ms. Gao and what was to happen to her.

"Prior to being moved, Ms. Gao was placed in a body bag in the darkened rear part of the room. Another dead person, a John Doe, from the hospital morgue was then put in her bed and transported by the Hong Kong Embassy helicopter and their crew. There were two assassins masquerading as medical assistants on the flight. Their plan was once they arrived on the Blue Ridge and after the helo departed, they were to move her to your sick bay. They were then to kill Ms. Gao and jump overboard. Others would have been possibly killed or at least badly wounded.

"Ms. Gao, in the body bag, instead was transported to a private mortuary where she is recovering nicely. Once she resumes consciousness, we will find out who beat her up. We will then have a key piece of the puzzle. The surface-to-air missile was as much a surprise to us as I am sure it was to them. It was launched by someone else who also knew she lived. The assassins were to be picked up by that boat, we feel. It is my feeling that it is either the Hong Kong Ambassador or CIA operative that were there the night we called CINCPACFLT from the embassy SCIF. I'm sorry if this offends you, but the guilty party might even be your U.S. Ambassador. Admiral, you must please not speak to anyone at all of this. No one."

Admiral Stewart nodded deep in thought. He knew the gravity of this information.

Then to both officers the Admiral stated, "Mr. Hsu, while I can appreciate your revelation, I am concerned at what happened in the harbor. This has endangered both the crew and ship as well as innocent by-standers. Rest assured, I will speak to no one of the issues you told me."

Then pausing, he said, "I have to go into Hong Kong for another evening activity and both ambassadors and the aforementioned CIA chief will be there. I will watch my comments."

He then looked directly at Spoke. "Pretty low blow you pulled Mister, but I guess I needed the reality check." Then as he started out the door he mumbled, "Damned Spooks."

Out in the passageway, he forced a smile at a startled passing steward and also his Flag LT. Then turned to the two intelligence officers, "I guess the Mike boat wasn't the most luxurious ride you've had coming out. If you can fit me into your busy schedule, and can wait about an hour, I'll give you a ride back in the barge."

The Admiral's Barge was like a very comfortably appointed cabin cruiser. Luxuriously trimmed in teak and mahogany with beautiful brass inlays and fixtures. It was heated and very comfortable.

Fang all but grabbed him and kissed his feet. From the sounds on the deck above them, the rain had increased as had the wind. Riding back even into the wind-driven swells would be so much better in a warm, dry and enclosed cabin.

Fang wanted to go to the mortuary, but was sure an hour would not make any difference. When his office communicated with him, the duress code word had not been used. Everything must be satisfactory.

"Admiral, is it alright if we use the Ship's Company Lounge while we wait?" Marks asked as the Admiral walked away. They only had "escort required" badges.

"Yes. And if anyone asks, tell them I'm escorting you," was the Admiral's retort. The trailing steward smiled and led them down the passageway to the lounge door.

CHAPTER 26 – THE DRUG SHIPMENT

The ride back was rough, but at least dry and warm. Fang was impressed with the Admiral's barge. He figured that if he was ever to join the U.S. Navy, he would insist on coming in as an Admiral with his own barge and boat crew. The arrival at the landing went without incident and both Fang and Spoke thanked the Admiral promising to keep him posted.

As the Admiral turned away, he addressed his comment to Spoke, "Mr. Marks, to avoid any pitfalls, report directly to me." His Flag LT, LT Eric Johnson nodded and winked at Spoke but said nothing.

Spoke understood completely. The rift with CDR Forner was obvious and he was glad the Admiral saw it clearly as well. Fang's interest was also greatly satisfied.

"It looks like your CINCPACFLT Admiral Donophan straightened out Admiral Stewart. I'm really glad we don't dance with the elephants. It's bad enough to have to smell the parts I have shoved in my face from my own world," Fang confided. Spoke smiled and nodded.

"We need to go up to the office," Fang said refusing to respond to his urges to go to the mortuary.

Back at the underground parking lot, the rain continued to come straight down. Spoke was glad they were somewhat protected from the wet.

RADM Stewart was headed for the Hong Kong Ambassador's home without CDR Forner, but he did have his Flag Lieutenant . LT Johnson was a good guy, but definitely was not in the "inner circle" and now with CDR Forner apparently no longer on the inside, things might go a bit smoother as far as communicating. At least Spoke would feel more comfortable about keeping his end up regarding developments as they occurred.

Inside the office, there was a note with the simple cover sheet "Imperial Hammer" on Fang's desk. Fang opened it and had a look of concern.

"Seems we have another drug shipment in Aberdeen tonight," he said. "Soon Wa wants us to meet him at the Tai Pak Restaurant in Aberdeen as quickly as we can get there. With rain, the roads might be a bit tricky. We need to get going right away."

The roads were indeed wet, but the rain seemed to let up on the other side of the island as they approached Aberdeen. The clouds hung low with occasional spots of drizzle. That low weather ceiling seemed to amplify sounds and smells of life in an aquatic city. Smells of cooking food, rancid rotting garbage, diesel fumes, decaying sea weed, human and animal waste and stale alcohol and tobacco smoke from bars that lined the harbor assaulted the nose. Sounds of fog horns, boat whistles, babies crying, occasional fights and car horns also proved that there were people all over – lots of people. Perhaps out of sight, but not out of mind.

Aberdeen's transient population lived chiefly in small sampans and junks. Generation after generation of families lived, loved, were born and died in this floating menagerie. Businesses, chiefly restaurants also thrived there. The Tai Pak was one of them.

The Tai Pak Restaurant was world renown as the location for the movie "Suzie Wong" and was a favorite gathering spot regardless of time or the day of the week for tourists and the wealthy in Hong Kong. Having it be a drop site for a large drug shipment was more than likely not accurate, but if the area was nearby, it would be far easier to use the crowds at the restaurant to hide from the law enforcement operatives. The down side was that it also would cover lookouts from the bad guys.

The Narcs from the police as well as the three INTERPOL agents had to blend in. That was a large order. It seems everyone could pick out police undercover agents. It was virtually a national sport to spot them and avoid them. Pickpockets, drug dealers as well as human traffickers could "smell" a cop even before they could get close. This would be a significant challenge.

There were always crowds that frequented the Tai Pak. This fact was universally well known. Another consideration by the smugglers was that since the restaurant was a floating restaurant, the general area was an ideal location for a drop. It was very difficult for the cops to sneak up on any covert activity. The smugglers also used the adage that hiding in plain sight was the easiest way to fool the cops.

Spoke knew all about the Top Secret operation "Imperial Hammer." He was "read in" and had already participated in phases of it. The operation was unknown except at the highest levels at MACV, Interpol and the Joint Chiefs of Staff at the Pentagon.

Special Operations units were infiltrating the heroin production facilities in the Golden Triangle and covertly planting small transmitters about the size of a small fat kindergarten crayon into bales of raw heroin. The transmitter's new NiCad batteries had a life of about six weeks and powered the small transmitters. This signal was specific to the receiving source which was tuned to the frequency. Now instead of tracking the myriads of small boats passing off the drugs to each other, they could just track the individual bales of material using a radio signal.

Tonight was the first time anyone knew that a marked bale had reached Hong Kong. This was the acid test. INTERPOL would be standing by to advise the Hong Kong Police. The Hong Kong Police would be the receiving party and tasked with capturing both drugs and traffickers.

Spoke had helped engineer some of the SEAL team's ops into Laos and farther north and west. He'd like to think his contributions made a difference. His relationship with his SEAL team had earned him a special spot in their minds and in their hearts. While totally off the books, Spoke had been invited to go with the team on several long range missions. He'd been witness to the insertion of the transmitters at the production sites.

He'd spent weeks living with Hmong villagers as had the rest of the team. While not exactly going native, he'd certainly gained a great respect for the Hmong people both as soldiers and fighters and family-centered people. It was one of the chief reasons why the Viet Cong and North Vietnamese hated them so much. They could not make inroads into the village life and tear apart the familial ties short of out and out killing them, often in grotesque ways.

Spoke waited just outside the Tai Pak with Fang. His mind cleared itself of past memories as the operation began to unfold. Numerous people milled around in the waiting line. Spoke knew they weren't all there for the cuisine, even though it was delicious. All law enforcement assets were professional and very discrete, obviously none wearing a uniform.

Fang's radio crackled in his ear piece. "Small boat approaching south of your position heading parallel to the restaurant's long side along the adjacent finger pier," the disembodied voice whispered.

Fang watched the small sampan turn off its small dual cylinder diesel engine and glide quietly to the adjacent finger pier. The crucial move now was to wait until the crew unloaded its cargo and didn't spook or head back into the black numerous surrounding boats. If they dropped the drugs into the harbor and headed back into the inky darkness, half their work would be worthless. They needed to capture not only the drugs, but also the mules and hopefully the next several rungs up the ladder.

Spoke sensed the tenseness in his partner's body language. Several couples started strolling up the pier toward shore, laughing and talking about how good the food was. A small Datsun cargo van labeled with Fresh Vegetables in Chinese characters and painted logo sat quietly with its engine and lights off at the head of the adjacent finger pier. As the sampan tied up starboard side to the pier, one of the two occupants in the boat stepped back and ducked into the small makeshift shelter.

Two men stepped out of the van and strolled down the finger pier. They walked past the sampan and appeared not to be interested in it or its cargo. Nothing happened. They continued talking and laughing as they worked their way toward the end of the finger pier.

The two van occupants reached the end of the finger pier and smoked a cigarette. Turning around they sauntered back toward shore.

The harbor night sounds were punctuated by the disemboweled boat horns, music and laughter from several bars and restaurants as well as the Tai Pak. A bottle broke and a fight broke out at a bar at the head of the pier. Two disgruntled bar occupants had been encouraged to take their dispute outside by the bar's bouncer. Verbal taunts and more broken bottles punctuated the night air. One did not have to speak Chinese to recognize what was happening.

Fang and Spoke were not taken in by the distraction. Each had been the author of too many diversions preceding serious operations. They knew what they were looking for and stayed vigilant.

The van occupants returned toward shore. When they got about 10 yards from the stern of the boat, a gunshot sounded near the head of the pier not far from the fight. This diversion had really gotten serious. Several women screamed, but the plain-clothes narcotics police knew not to react or blow their cover. Crowd reaction was important, and it was expected that this would occur.

Then Fang saw what he was looking for. The sampan occupant lifted the tarp at the bow end of the makeshift cabin and lifted two cube-like shapes onto the pier. He was reaching for a third when a second gunshot echoed in the night. People began running away from the finger pier screaming.

The two van occupants picked up the bales and ran toward the van. The sampan crewman then lifted a third cube shape and put it on the pier. People scattered at the head of the pier. In the confusion, the men appeared to fit in. After reaching the van, the driver jumped in and started the van. The helper turned and raced back down the pier to the third bale.

Picking it up, the helper turned and started running toward the van. The driver of the van had backed the van out and was racing the engine encouraging his buddy to hurry. As the helper reached the open side door of the van, four plain-clothes policemen jumped in front and to the side of the van with weapons drawn.

The driver demonstrated an absolute determination to avoid being apprehended. He stepped on the gas and started the van in motion. One officer fired a round into the engine block and another fired into the tire. From point blank range there was little chance of ricochet or of missing. Four additional policemen raced down the finger pier to the sampan before the startled crew could push off. By the time Fang and Spoke arrived, the party had pretty well concluded - no more fireworks and no casualties.

The "take" would later turn out to be about $28,000,000 worth of raw China White heroin. This appeared as three burlap encased canvas and plastic wrapped bales. Fang was positive it would not be vegetables for local restaurants.

One thing worried him though, no one else moved either to intercede or to attempt rescue of the shipment. In the excitement of the bust, there was no "extra baggage" to explain the unexplainable. Yet, there were eyes watching what happened. Eyes that would not forget faces nor would they forgive the intrusion into their world.

CHAPTER 27 – CHANGE OF VENUE

INTERPOL Headquarters, Hong Kong

Paper work, the bane of all operations and field operatives, even international counter-drug work. Someday someone would develop a way to make the reporting paperwork just magically go away. Spoke had to contact the Admiral at once. A telephone call to the Embassy would be in order.

"American Embassy," the switchboard operator routinely announced.

"Is Rear Admiral Stewart still there?" Spoke asked with as little emotion as he could muster.

"One moment, sir, I'll check."

After a few minutes, a voice announced, "This is LT Johnson."

"Eric, Marks. I have to speak immediately to the Admiral."

"I'll get him." LT Johnson's voice took on the immediacy of the situation and the gravity of the moment. Time stood still as Marks held his breath. Breathe, breathe he kept saying to himself. Finally, the familiar voice came on the line.

"Admiral Stewart."

"Emergency at the harbor landing, sir. Your presence is requested immediately," responded Spoke as officially as possible. "Time is of the essence."

"I'll be there in less than 20 minutes," the Admiral responded quickly. He motioned to LT Johnson to get his car and raincoat and hat. He'd make his apologies to the Ambassador and guests.

Shore Patrol Headquarters, Quay Wall parking area, Hong Kong

Admiral Stewart arrived with his driver and Flag Lieutenant. He directed his driver and LT Johnson to remain at the vehicle. He walked over to LT Marks and Mr. Hsu. "We've got to stop meeting like this, Mr. Marks. Good evening, Mr. Hsu?"

Fang responded quietly, "Good evening, Admiral. Sorry to ruin your evening."

Spoke followed quickly with, "Sir, when we returned to the INTERPOL office this evening, we were alerted that an Imperial Hammer drug shipment was arriving in Aberdeen this evening. We were there when the shipment was confiscated. There were three bales, approximately $28,000,000 of raw, uncut heroin. The Hong Kong Police have them now. They also have the crew of the boat and the two men who tried to receive the shipment. This is going to really shake up whoever wanted those drugs."

"Excellent. How is Ms. Gao? I believe that is her name."

Fang responded quietly, "We don't know yet. We were going there after we finished talking with you."

"Thank you, Mr. Hsu. I sincerely hope she is doing better. You two have become an amazing team. Unfortunately, I'm going to rain on your parade. After your call to me, I received a call from CINCPACFLT. When you return from seeing Ms. Gao, Mr. Marks you will be heading for Yokosuka, Japan. CINCPACFLT has ordered you on another assignment. You are not to go to your hotel room. You are to immediately get to the International Airport. Your orders and additional tickets will be waiting for you in Yokosuka."

The Admiral stared into two sets of disbelieving eyes. What could be more important than saving public lives against this hideous drug? The startled look on both faces almost made the Admiral laugh. To maintain decorum, however, he turned and walked over to his car and motioned to his Flag LT and driver to head for the barge.

Fang and Spoke got into the car and drove silently to the mortuary. Both felt that if they said anything, even more bad karma would befall them. They'd grown really close in the few days, less than a week, they'd worked together. Neither knew when or even if they'd ever see each other again. Spoke knew these kinds of situations were what military life meant, but it still wasn't easy. Spoke had the same feelings toward members of the SEAL Team he worked with in Vietnam.

They arrived at the mortuary and quietly walked inside. It was dark as they made their way to the rear of the chapel. The door to the rear was also dark. This had the wrong feeling. Fang drew his revolver.

Closely they walked to the back, feeling for the door handle, adrenaline rising and giving each an all-to-familiar, overbearing metallic taste in their mouths. Carefully they opened the door. Their eyes had become accustomed to the dark and the soft glow at the bottom of the opposite door became clear. Fang moved toward the door with all senses at full alert. He carefully opened the door.

In the dim light, Fang saw Mei-Li. She was there and quietly sleeping the drug induced sleep of recovery. The nurse motioned for quiet with her fingers against her mouth. Placing her semi-auto weapon down, she motioned Fang and Spoke to come closer.

"How's she doing?" Fang whispered.

"She's as good as can be expected. The doctor is asleep, but has promised she should be awake in the next day or so."

"Thank you. Please keep me informed as soon as she wakes," Fang said quietly. He turned and started toward the door they came in. "And please, tell Dr. Fu, thank you for going out of his way with this one." She smiled and nodded.

Outside, Fang said to Spoke. "Get me a way to contact you. I'll let you in on the details as they develop."

"I don't want to compromise anything you are doing, but I will give you my word, I will help any way I can," responded Spoke.

"Thank you. It is my honor to have served and to continue to serve with you, my friend."

CHAPTER 28 – TOP SECRET OP

"It's good to be king," Yeoman Master Chief Ramsey chuckled.

"The Admiral called and asked that you be patient. He said he'd be a few minutes more. He's with a group of Navy League wives from Dallas, TX, and they had a few questions."

Marks sat down and looked around at the office. Little had changed in almost 8 months since he'd left for South Vietnam. The Admiral had a great collection of hats. It was his visual way of demonstrating that he frequently wore many hats. His flight helmet sat on top clearly representing his personal crowning achievement, but he had at least 45 hats from ball caps to a chef's toque.

The best visual image, however, still resided in the corner where it had been before - a large stone with a two-handed Claymore sword and plaque indicating its name was Excalibur.

Marks turned and observed Master Chief Ramsey busily cleaning up and straightening his desk.

"When did you pin on Master Chief?" Marks asked. "I thought you refused to kiss anyone's alternative appendages when it came to advancement."

"Now you sound like my ex-wife, my wife, my girlfriend and my kids. Actually, the Navy came to its senses about two weeks ago and conferred the blessed event effective the 1st of March. By the way, the last time I saw you, you were a sniveling "JG" still trying to find the coffee maker for the Admiral."

"Well it proves both of us are sneaky and underhanded. When do you get paid for your high and exalted achievement?" Marks responded smiling broadly, his eyes twinkling.

"Now you really do sound like my ex- and my wife. BUPERS says another 4 to 6 months. By then they hope I'll have forgotten about it. Anyway Lieutenant, you know, this is the modern Navy. We do it for the adventure, not the pay!" Master Chief paused and his tone and demeanor changed - sobering dramatically. "How was it? Vietnam, I mean. The boss said you were in some rough stuff over there."

"Master Chief, war truly is hell. I did make some very close and long-lasting friends. I owe my life to many. In fact, I think that's why I'm here now."

"Well, sir, you have my vote for *the best officer* I've ever had the privilege of working with."

"Master Chief, you can't even imagine how much that means to me. I met some really great people, but you and the boss are without a doubt, men I'd gladly give my life for."

Both stopped short of getting teary-eyed and none too soon. The Admiral's Flag Lieutenant, LT James Barker came in the door and all but threw his hat at the outer office hat tree. "Damn! If I hear one more of those bittys ask one more stupid question! I don't know how he does it!

Master Chief rolled his eyes, "It's why he gets paid the big bucks, Sir. '*Beware the Ides of March.*'"

Then spotting Marks, Barker said, "Spoke! Look at you..... and the railroad tracks!"

Railroad tracks indicated the insignia of a Lieutenant in the Navy and Coast Guard. The same insignia referred to a Captain in the Army, Air Force and Marine Corps.

Turning to the Master Chief, Barker continued, "My how quickly our little ones get big. You send them out into the big bad world and they come back all "growed up." Let's go out soon and catch up," his voice dripping with condescension.

Marks didn't like him when he was stationed there at CINCPACFLT and time hadn't improved anything. Barker had arrived as the Flag Lieutenant almost two years ago. His attitudes and mannerisms made the fun of the CINCPACFLT assignment every junior officer's worst nightmare. He was little more than a condescending jerk. He was so jealous when Admiral Donophan had taken Marks under his wing. Barker had all but singled out Marks for a personal vendetta. The Master Chief turned away and when Barker turned his back to him, gave Marks the "finger in the mouth" gag sign. Marks just smiled.

The Admiral came through the doors and gave a glowing smile when he recognized LT Marks.

"Kevin! It is great to see you! Come into my office." Turning to the Flag Lieutenant he said, "Get me a cup of coffee, black and strong. LT, a cup for you?"

"No thanks, Admiral," was the smiling, confident but lower toned reply.

"Oh that's right, you haven't been corrupted yet by Naval traditions." Marks knew that Admiral Donophan was only teasing him. He also knew that one of the reasons Marks was there was because of the high set of standards he lived by.

Marks also remembered the only time he'd ever had to make coffee for the office. He'd come in at 0500 and after finally finding the coffee pot, he stood facing it wondering what to do next. Since he'd never made coffee before, he put in the water, placed the filter in the top basket and then filled the basket full of coffee grounds – about ½ a can. He turned it on and let it perk. At that time, he wondered how coffee lovers ever made it with nothing less than a semi-truck full of coffee cans if it took that much coffee to perk one pot.

When everyone started coming in that morning, then Senior Chief Ramsey, went to grab his first cup. He commented before drinking it that it sure looked black and smelled strong, "Just the way the Admiral likes it, strong and hot." Of course, that first sip sent him right up the wall. After that it was a Chinese fire drill, all asses and elbows, trying to get a fresh pot made up in time for the Admiral's arrival. After that, Marks never had to make coffee again. Seems everyone always volunteered to do it for him.

They closed the door and sat down after the Flag Lieutenant left. The Admiral moved over to the couch from his desk motioning Marks to sit across from him in a large overstuffed leather chair.

Settled, he asked, "How was it?" He'd been a combat ace in Korea and again in early Vietnam. He knew the fear and terror one felt when faced with death and the horror of combat. He'd watched the eyes of pilots he fought against as he shot down their planes.

"Admiral, I won't lie, it was rough at times. The guys with SEAL Team are some fantastic friends. My very short tour in Hong Kong also had some amazing things happen. I also made a couple of awesome and lifelong friends. I'm sure Admiral Stewart has included you on most of them. I really wanted to stay."

"I understand and yes, Admiral Stewart did mention what you accomplished." Marks sensed Admiral Donophan really did understand.

"Kevin, I'm going to level with you. What I am about to tell you is Top Secret. I pulled you out of Hong Kong because you'd been compromised and there is now a contract out on your life. You are hereby banned from Hong Kong until told otherwise. It seems there are some political powers that have tried to muscle in on the Triad's drug smuggling. The contract is from a political power not the Triads. INTERPOL moved Mr. Hsu to Taipei along with Ms. Gao. She is alive, continuing to recover nicely and has identified her attackers. The dominoes have begun to fall there. It seems there are implications all the way up to the Hong Kong Ambassador and the Red Chinese government."

He stopped to allow the message to sink in. "There is another urgent need and this comes all the way from SECNAV. He has tasked me to find an operative that can locate a group of people.

"Seems our Under Secretary of the Navy, Mike Mahoney's daughter was kidnapped. There is extremely strong evidence that she and some other young white girls are victims of a kidnap and slave smuggling scheme in Southeast Asia for some of the drug lords there. It doesn't appear to be a targeted kidnap; instead one of random opportunity. I was asked to choose a team to hopefully find these girls and their kidnappers.

"You and SEAL Team One were selected due in part to your knowledge of the lay of the land there. The other reason was frankly I trust you and know you'll be successful. SECNAV does not agree. He's already lost two Naval Investigative Service agents getting what we know.

"FBI offered as did CIA. Neither was acceptable. SECNAV, however, was really leery of sending in the SEAL Team cavalry to play cowboys and Indians with the locals. I assured him you are not that kind of operative. I also contacted CAPT Geary, Ops and Commander of the SEALS under Rear Admiral Stewart.

"He queried LCDR Rogers who said if they had anyone to run point as their intelligence officer, it was you. You are making a lot of people very happy with your work, young man. Your dad and granddad would be really proud. All of you will be briefed in Perth, Australia, next Tuesday aboard the Blue Ridge."

Another pause to let Marks think about what had been said. "Concerns, problems, questions?" Again a pause.

"Just one. Will I have time to make Mongolian BBQ at Tripler tonight?" Both men smiled and Admiral Donophan started laughing.

Tripler Army Hospital had the best Mongolian BBQ on Oahu at the Officers Club and it was every Wednesday night. It was the night of nights for dining out. If you were anybody, you didn't miss that event of the week.

"Is there a straight bone in your body, Marks? You're just like your old man. Master Chief will get your airline tickets, allotments and Page 2 updates done. Make sure you finish them. I understand that last time there were some omissions before you went in-country. Medical will also want to give you the mandatory shots and piss in the bottle. By the way how's your family?"

"My family is fine. I miss the heck out of the kids, but I know they'll be strong enough to do alright. They come from great genes. If problems occur, my sister Marilyn will help. Charlene is going through more of her depressions. Marilyn has power of attorney to take the kids if I say so, and I just might. I'll get with Master Chief right away and make sure everything is in order with JAG as well."

"I'm truly sorry about your personal problems, LT, but if you feel it will compromise your ability to do this, I'll get someone else."

"Admiral, I need the success. Not only will I do it, I'll do it to the standard of excellence you expect," Marks replied sincerely.

"I know you will. Just remember, LT, this is all Top Secret. No one knows what is up including this office except you and me. Your cover story is that you are just going on a well-deserved leave."

"Yes, sir."

CHAPTER 29 - REUNION

1000, USS Blue Ridge (LCC-19), Perth, Australia

The Admiral's Briefing Theater aboard Blue Ridge was familiar territory. Even though it had been three weeks before, it seemed like only yesterday. Marks walked in. The Marine Corporal standing in the passageway closed the door. CAPT Ralph Geary, Assistant Chief of Staff for Operations and hands-on director of SEALs for CTF 76; CAPT Dick Mortensen, CTF 76 Chief of Staff; CAPT Robert Bowen, CO of the Blue Ridge; LCDR Randy Rogers, SEAL Team One, Detachment B team leader; and, in the back the familiar face of Mr. Hsu Feng Jyan all looked up from briefing folders as he walked in.

The look of excitement that filled Marks' eyes as he saw his old comrades was thunderous. He noticed at once the empty seat between Fang and Bee. Quickly he sat. Hand clasps under the edge of the table and smiles said volumes. Noticeably missing was CDR Forner, the Duck.

The door opened. "Attention on deck." All arose.

Rear Admiral Stewart walked in, "Gentlemen, thank you and please be seated. This entire briefing is Top Secret. Nothing is to leave this room and is not to be discussed with anyone other than those in this room. Mr. Hsu is with INTERPOL and definitely is cleared to be here. Mr. Hsu, welcome."

"Thank you, Admiral."

Admiral Stewart continued, "Gentlemen, two weeks ago a young woman, a child, was kidnapped in Anacostia, Maryland. She is no different from many thousands of other children forced into the wretched world of child prostitution except she is the daughter of Navy Undersecretary Mike Mahoney. This has not only Navy interest, but the White House also.

"In front of you is the information from SECNAV, CINCPACFLT, DIA, CIA, FBI and NIS. This information plus the bios of other known abducted children in the general area of Anacostia in that week and their families are all we have at the moment. There have been no ransom demands for any of these abductions. This is why the FBI has been ordered off the case until we can give them more info. They apparently do not have a deep enough foreign cadre staff anyway. They will, however, have a liaison assigned to CINCPACFLT's staff to monitor our progress in Saigon. SECNAV insists it is our jurisdiction anyway and wants no part of CIA involvement.

"That being said he is under the gun from the State Department not to turn this into a Wild West Shoot-Out. The White House has given us 90 days before they interject State and the whole thing goes public, and I might add, goes to hell in a hand-basket. Keeping a lid on this makes hiding the nuclear football codes look like the Easter Egg Roll at the White House – all a jumbled up mess. I don't want the Navy looking like the cause of any problems.

"Now take a few minutes and look over the information. As you can see, the locating information from informants in Southeast Asia pinpoints an area near the Laotian border. Several drug lords were spotted having recent additions of Anglo children added to their harems."

Each man continued to regard his respective folder. Each folder was created to assist that particular member of the team. Blue Ridge's Intelligence Department had their fingerprints all over the data and the report. Spoke's folder was the largest, closely followed by Bee's. Spoke wanted to meet with both Fang and Bee together, alone. They each needed to know the other and what each brought to the table. Both were invaluable and yet "inter-valuable" at the same time. Each had key pieces to a puzzle that could unlock critical doors and the solution of this nightmare.

Human smuggling and child slave prostitution had been going on for myriads of centuries. They could not stop it. They would not dent the corrupt, sick minds that robbed families and children of their lives. They would not put an end to the hell each day brought to those forced into the drug-induced stranglehold. Nor would they dent the sex abuse imposed on fragile lives. Each horror took away a child's childhood leaving only the dark nightmares their lives would have forever. Spoke thought of his kids. How would he react if it was his child? What would he tell others about what he did to prevent it or avenge their kidnapping?

His mind was forcibly brought back to the present with the Admiral asking for any questions. None were immediately voiced.

Admiral Stewart then indicated that he would reconvene the meeting at 0800 the next morning. He expected each person to review the information in their folders and for CAPT Geary and his team to have a plan, but cautioned them that the folders were *not* to leave the room. He also reminded them that this operation was Top Secret.

All stood as he departed. The Chief of Staff and CO of the Blue Ridge also departed after the Admiral.

CAPT Geary, a SEAL also, then turned to the remaining three and said, "Gentlemen, as you can see, this comes from the highest centers of power in the Western World. It has the eyes of the Commander and Chief.

"SECNAV feels we can't do it. I don't care how, but we will do it and do it with honor. Be ready to brief tomorrow morning with your plan.

"Mr. Hsu, I'm sure you have an understanding of the military order of things and how we do them in our world. Please respect LCDR Rogers. He is the team captain on this op and the one whose ass is on the line. Best get to work."

Then to LCDR Rogers, "Randy, whatever you need, let me know. I'll be in OPS." OPS was the heart of the ship. Blue Ridge was technically not a surface combatant, but she still had both an Operations Center and a Combat Center. She could mount point defense with her 3" gun mounts, as well as direct the landing force ashore and collect many, many kinds of intelligence. Essentially she was a covert intelligence-gathering platform on steroids, not to mention a floating hotel, hospital and intelligence center.

CAPT Geary rose and departed.

The three men faced each other and even though they realized the gravity of the situation, they could not stop big smiles and handshakes. Spoke felt he'd been invited to play on the Dream Team.

"How's Mei-Li?" was the first thing out of Spoke's mouth. He was like a little kid wanting an ice cream cone, and wanting it now!

"She is doing much better," Fang responded.

"She finally came around two days after you left. An attempt was made on my life going into work the next afternoon. My boss ordered me to leave as soon as possible. I told him I had to wait until Mei-Li was strong enough to travel. She would be coming with me. He ordered us to a safe house in Kowloon. We had to wait 6 more days, but flew to Taipei and then to another safe house outside of Taipei. She is still there, but sends her regards. We are headed for Kaohsiung. I have additional details I can provide to our operation."

"Spoke, please do more than just give me his name," said Bee. Thrusting out his hand he said, "I'm LCDR Randy Rogers. I'm the Team Leader of SEAL Team One Det B. My guys call me Bee, but for the world I don't know why."

Spoke smiled sheepishly, "Bee, meet Mr. Hsu Feng Jyan. He prefers to have his associates call him Fang. He was my mentor and guide, not to mention my lifesaver in Hong Kong. Both of you have saved my life. Like you, I owe him a lot. It's time I pay both of you back. And how is Sandy? Are you still a thing?"

Rogers smiled, shook Fang's hand and said, "Sandy's fine and yes, we are still doing our thing, even though it's not as often as we like. Now, let's get down to business. Fang what do we know about the areas we've been given in our briefing books?"

CHAPTER 30 – THE PLAN
FOR RECOVERY

"Gentlemen, that concludes our briefing. Are there any questions, additions or things you feel we've forgotten?" LCDR Rogers asked the assembled cadre.

"Timeline again," asked CAPT Geary.

His logistics line was crucial to making sure the support, the insertion, the extraction and the cover story were impeccable. He was the P.R. and logistics side of CINCPACFLT's operation as well as the next head on the block after LCDR Rogers' if things went bad.

LCDR Rogers began, "The team will be nine hand-picked men including LT Marks and Mr. Hsu. We are inserted at Chiang Rai, Thailand. The area is only quasi friendly to us and so this must be at night and under cover of darkness. Mr. Hsu's Interpol contact will meet us at Chiang Saen where we will cross into Laos. The local warlord will provide cover with prepaid agreements. Obviously it will be conditional arrangements with payments provided only when we get out. Their motivation besides the dollars is obvious in that if we remove his opponent we help him."

The age-old cliché of "the enemy of my enemy is my friend" was alive and well and embodied in this operation.

"We will be in-country for five days. Our objective has been photographed as a possible site. No confirmation as to who or how many there are, but it is known for drug production, packaging and human trafficking, mostly young girls, but a few boys too. A fresh shipment arrived early yesterday according to the rival warlord's informant who gave us these photos and the information. He said there were a number of white, Anglo or European blonde and red-headed girls matching the general description of our target. He was sure the area was being used as a training location for prostitutes for Bangkok and several other places controlled by this particular warlord. The way they keep these children under control is through drug addiction and drumming into their minds that there is no hope of escape. For the first while, the captors keep them very well attended-to medically, but deny them food. So our children probably will be good and hungry. They also have limited contact with everyone except their female handlers who have been through the same treatment all their teen and adult lives. This may pose some issues for extraction, but again hopefully we can persuade them to change their lifestyles.

"Photos show several possible ways for ingress and egress. LT Marks has come up with a diversionary operation involving some pyro-techniques, lots of noise and potentially lots of bullets aimed downrange away from the captives. He has a list of things he will need. The volume of the pyro techniques may pose some challenges during our ingress, but if it does the job, it will save a lot of lives.

"Mr. Hsu will engage the guards as the diversion is underway. We are counting on his language skills to get us through the barriers we face to extract the children. The numbers of children given by the informant mean we will be slowed down significantly and we will need to be extracted quickly. No doubt we will need a Jolly Green to get us out as well as a gun ship or two, most certainly with at least CAP support."

Gun ships would be Huey Cobras and CAP referred to overhead jets, fast fliers, from Thailand to keep Laotian Air Force aircraft away.

"Contact frequency once we are clear of the objective and link up both squads will signal the need for our support. Laotian Air Force should not be a factor but shoulder fired surface to air missiles are. The Triads still have an interest here, not to mention the Red Chinese. It is not clear who is really behind this particular drug/kidnapping operation.

"With all of the issues to prepare for, we would like to have wheels up from Nakhon Phanom in 96 hours. Are there any questions?"

With no further questions, the meeting adjourned, the key players remained confirming once again any questions and objectives. Now it was time for boots to hit the trail.

CHAPTER 31 – LAOS, AGAIN

0300, Nakhon Phanom, Thailand

It was miserably hot. Humidity was close to 97% and even at "oh-dark-thirty" it was 86-degrees. Current issue rip-stop, camouflage uniforms were not the most comfortable in that environment. Spoke kept thinking that whoever designed these things needed to wear them in full combat web gear and have 100-pounds of weight on their back in a jungle environment. Then maybe they would choose a different design and choice of cloth. He was surprised they didn't have thermal underwear sewn in and down padding in each garment. There must have been some mistake when the military supply centers got orders for South East Asia. Some "brain trust" must have misread the request and thought it said South East Alaska.

Naturally, the first thing off was the shirt. Even the sleeveless green undershirts and olive drab T-shirts seemed hot. Every garment was already drenched in sweat.

Each man also had a nylon mesh hooded shirt to make indigenous coverings – ghillie suits – for themselves when they got to the area of operations. This had become an almost essential piece of operational gear for long range recon units as well as special operations teams.

Besides their web gear, each carried enough ammo for the operation plus a little extra. Each man also carried a Fairbairn-Sykes fighting stiletto; without doubt, the tool everyone wanted when the action was "in close and personal."

The knife's design had existed since before World War II with the British SAS. It lasted that long because it worked. It had saved Spoke's life and those he was with at the time.

They each had two canteens, a first aid pack and emergency straws. The straws had filters that removed virtually every bug and chemical, but the filter life was not known to be especially long in the brackish waters they would be traveling in. They tended to clog, so these would be used first and then buried. The canteens would be used second.

Spoke carried his favorite weapon, a suppressed MAC-10 in .45 caliber as well as seven 32-round magazines in a Chinese chest ammo carrier. The rest of the team always laughed, saying he wanted to "look bad guys in the eye" before unleashing hell on them.

Spoke never said much about it, but hoped he would never have to use it at all. Still, as he said, he had proven his skill with the weapon and was really good with it.

The MAC was one heck of a room-sweeping party crasher. No one could dispute that fact. Numerous times he'd gone to the range and won bet after bet before there were no more takers except for "newbies." Not that he actually bet, except for maybe a ginger ale, but everyone smiled when he had a new sucker on the line.

Spoke had become quite a connoisseur of ginger ale. Since being in the Far East he'd tasted them all. His favorite was San Miguel. So much so that the guys in the Supply Department put in a stock of the stuff at the club just for Spoke.

Everyone else on the team carried suppressed M-16s, except for Fang who could not seem to replace his AK-47. He professed that since the bad guys probably had them, he could get by with their ammo and he would not have to carry the extra weight. Spoke couldn't fault his argument, but he still loved his MAC.

Once inside Laos, with a quick march, they could get to their area of operations in approximately 30 hours. That meant they had to have what they needed on their back. No overnight bivouacs, nothing other than brief rests. This had to be a lightning strike – once in country, the "jungle drums would be talking."

The success of their operation depended on the speed, quietness and effectiveness of their movement. It also depended on the greed and animosity of the bad guys' enemy. This is what they were building an entire operation on not to mention staking the team's lives and the lives of these children on.

The team gathered for one last briefing prior to departure. Each man checked their fellow team mates gear for potential problems. It was almost meaningless, except that it calmed each member of the team. These men were professional and not one was a beginner at covert operations.

No op was ever simple. No op was easy. The SEAL slogan of "the only easy day was yesterday" was just as important on this op as any other they'd ever done. Each man knew the lives of these children were in their hands not to mention their teammates and their own lives.

Bee then turned the last formal briefing to Spoke. Spoke pulled out a map and several pictures of the compound.

"We will be feet dry at this point. We have 30 hours to be in position here. Once we arrive, Bee, Mr. Hsu and the Fire Team will spread out on the East side of the camp closest to the holding huts. The Expo Team and I will move to the closest point near the main entrance of the compound." Here he pointed to the pictures of the compound and the road/trail entering the village.

"At the appointed time, we will give the surprise of the century to some very unsuspecting viewers. Thirty seconds after the start of this, Mr. Hsu will then confront the remaining guards over at the hut holding the hostages.

"The Fire Team will follow and recover the prisoners.

"Egress is then to the South one mile to this point."

Spoke pointed to the point on the map and diagram of the compound and then to the picture they had of the same area.

"Rendezvous with the Fire Team and the Expo Team will happen at this point," he pointed at the map.

"We have 2 hours to get to point X-ray for full extraction via Jolly Green. Our window is small due to the response of the Laotian Air Force, however we have been assured that CAP and ground support will be complements of the 474th Fighter Wing from here at Udorn.

"Our biggest concern is the Jolly Green's time on station due to possible portable Chinese SAMs or RPGs which are rumored to be in the hands of the bad guys. Since they will not have fixed radar, Iron Hand missions will not be used or for that matter, available. We need to get in and get out fast."

Spoke knew all the men were familiar with Iron Hand missions which had been very successful since the late 60's. One aircraft would try to get painted by radar and another aircraft would launch a "beam rider" at the signal generation site.

Such missions had an extremely steep learning curve and the North Vietnamese had learned to paint the aircraft and then turn off the radar. The real concern would be if some of the bad guys had either been in Vietnam or trained by the Chinese or Soviets.

While RPGs were not new, man-portable Surface to Air missiles or SAMS were a relatively new wrinkle. If this was indeed state-sponsored drug production destined for the West, they would do just about anything to protect it.

"Let's synchronize our watches. Time is 0315.... mark!" Bee was anxious. This was a different type of operation than they were really used to. Normally, the age of the captives was considerably older. His concerns centered on how well the children would respond and function.

After checking each man, Bee looked around and motioned the team to move toward the unmarked C-47 aircraft just starting its warm-up. The venerable DC-3 or C-47 as the military dubbed it, would not appear out of place landing inland at Chiang Rai. The travel time would be about one and a half hours.

0440, Chiang Rai, Thailand

The C-47 landed hard and bounced its way down the remaining rough runway. Rising air currents and heat, especially after dark, can really mess up a flying object trying to land safely. Hopefully, this was just the pilot getting the butterflies out. It sure didn't help the passengers. All members looked at each other, each getting their emotions hardened up for the significant challenge ahead.

The aircraft taxied to the remote end of the runway much the same way it would if they were transferring "other products" discretely. They knew they were being watched and their presence monitored so this had to look perfectly normal, sort like contraband or at least drugs. They were to remain aboard until their next aircraft taxied over to them.

That next aircraft was a good bit smaller and already waiting for them in the dark.

"Are you sure this thing still flies?" Fang asked Spoke quietly with a very doubt-filled look.

"Well the Russians and the Chinese seem to think so." Spoke whispered back and smiled but his mind wondered the same thing.

The Russian-built AN-2 ("Annie") bi-winged aircraft carried discrete tail markings of a Laotian registered aircraft. It was the perfect cover since much of the drug traffic flowing out of Laos' remote airstrips and Thai strips for conveyance to the world were carried by AN-2's and other clones similar in appearance and characteristics. It carried the 10 men, nine of the team and the pilot, as well as their limited gear for this operation. Even if someone saw the AN-2 land in the Chiang Saen airstrip, it definitely would not appear out of place especially if it taxied to the remote part of the strip.

CHAPTER 32 – INGRESS AND SURPRISE

0500, Chiang Saen, Thailand

Spoke thought to himself that if someone had witnessed the unloading of the AN-2, it probably looked like the 20 clowns coming out of the mini car at the circus. That was the only humorous thought in his mind at this time.

The humidity was stifling and the air as fetid as the local landfill in the heat of summer. What a place, he thought. This has to be close to hell.

The team quickly moved to the perimeter of the strip and waited on the far side of the cleared land surrounding the airport.

A pinpoint flash of blue light gave Bee all the details he needed. He gathered the team quietly and moved toward the light source.

Their guide, Kaipo, appeared on cue. He motioned that they should follow him. They departed the airport and made their way toward the river separating Thailand and Laos.

Kaipo said nothing but motioned for them to move along the bank upstream. There were three, shallow-draft, canoe-type boats. They looked like mini Laotian Slow Boats but were only 18 or so feet long and without a cabin. The beams were super narrow and reminded Spoke of hollowed-out pencils. Each boat could hold four adults including gear and the boat operator, but the team managed to get into the three boats still leaving room for the guide.

The crossing was relatively uneventful. All of the team were prepared for anything, but knew that once into the dug-outs they had to move as little as possible to avoid swimming.

Spoke's load wasn't really heavy, just really large and bulky. Each of the men on the Expo Team also had huge packs. In this case, size did matter and the display they put on had to be convincing enough to not only turn heads, but draw them towards the action.

The air weighed a ton. The heat at 0700 was oppressive. Laos was no better a place than Thailand. Imagine that, thought Spoke. He laughed at his tired frame of mind.

The first puddle they came to, the straws came out. The water tasted lousy. For all he knew, the puddle was a water buffalo wallow. Whoever sold these pieces of junk to the military really sold them a bill of goods. The water stank, but it was better than losing all their moisture as sweat.

After five minutes, they continued on. Spoke noticed the change of scenery and flora as they did more climbing than descending. It appeared they were going higher up.

The pass or what felt like a pass was surrounded by higher hills. He was glad it wasn't karst which would have cut up their foot gear, but it still felt like a miserable workout that never seemed to end.

Karst was the lava soil that frequently had huge spires. Since the jungle had overgrown even the spires, the ground was seemingly littered with glass-like shards of reddish-black sand and pebbles.

18 hours into the endurance test, Bee finally called a halt. They would rest here. Each man knew the importance of rest and Fang and Spoke almost instantly fell asleep.

Bee organized a watch and conferred with Kaipo. He indicated they were over half way there. Bee watched as Kaipo sat and appeared to drop off.

Bee then moved over to Senior Chief LaMonde. Quietly he nudged him. The Senior Chief awoke and instantly was on the alert; too many ops where such a reaction was essential for remaining alive.

"What do you make of this so called guide?"

Senior Chief whispered, "I thought I was only tired and paranoid. He bothers me. There's something not quite right. We need to watch him closely. I'll go relieve Mitchell."

"Thanks, Senior. Check our guest as well."

Senior Chief LaMonde moved away silently. He pushed gently on Obermeyer's leg to signal he was next watch. The watches were only 30 minutes or so to allow as much rest time as possible for each man.

Then LaMonde moved to where Kaipo was supposed to be sleeping. He was gone.

LaMonde moved quickly to Bee. "He's gone."

Bee directed all to be awake.

"We have a problem," Bee whispered. "Let's move the team and watch this place. Hopefully, he only needed to make a head call and was a little shy."

Each man moved to a concealed position around their makeshift campsite. Spoke and Fang felt the intense, hot night envelope them.

If Kaipo had led them into a trap, they would fail at their operation and possibly lose the entire team. Since no one would know where they were, military archives would only list them as Missing in Action. What would happen to their families? Great time to think of that.

Time moved so slowly. Spoke tried to estimate seconds by holding his breath. He couldn't even concentrate to do that. Fang nudged him. Saying nothing he moved his eyes to the left a couple of times. Spoke saw it too. Three men appeared only as shadows against background foliage. Those men weren't any of the team.

The sound was almost imperceptible. "Americans, Americans," called the voice.

"This Kaipo. I bring help. Americans, Americans."

He moved to the most open place as a move of good faith. He laid down his AK-47 and stepped back from it.

Again he called, "Americans, Americans. I bring help. I not armed. We get bad people. I bring help."

He motioned for an invisible partner or partners to come to him and disarm. Five men stepped forward and laid down their AK-47s. Still everything remained quiet.

No one from the team moved or even tried to breathe. Bee made the first move. He quietly stood and moved toward the group. No one else moved. Bee approached them and motioned for the group to remain quiet. "Where did you go?"

Kaipo quietly replied, "Get more men. Need more men to take village."

Bee couldn't believe his ears. "What village?" he whispered incredulously.

"Village by camp."

As he said this, four more men materialized from the surrounding foliage. That gave the complete team a complement of 10 natives plus their own 9.

"How close are we to the camp?" asked Bee.

"8 hours if no bothered by spies," struggled Kaipo. He was having a more and more difficult time speaking English as the stress of the situation became more palpable.

Bee waited a few minutes to clear his mind and formulate a plan. He then raised his hand and his team materialized.

Bee moved over to Fang and Spoke. "We have a new wrinkle. Seems there is a village we weren't told about to start. Kaipo says he went for help. We now have 10 more men to use ..... and to deal with. The local double and triple canopy had concealed the additional village from our recon flights."

Spoke thought quickly. He turned to Fang. "Can you follow the language if one of their men, say Kaipo, works with you after the distraction starts?"

Fang nodded. Spoke then turned to Bee, "Skipper, what if we use the other 9 to augment our Expo Team? Maybe have them come in from the general area we mount our distraction. That will really force their hand on commitment to defense. We just need to know where the village huts are. If we use our Expo Team as before, but have the other 9 attack opposite the main group of huts, that way they will have to move to their response in the open. It solidifies the attack and makes our Expo more believable."

Bee thought for a moment and grabbed Kaipo and turned to Fang. "Fang, ask him what other surprises he has in store. Can you do it in his own language?"

Fang switched to Laotian. He quizzed Kaipo, but then said he had no other changes or surprises.

Bee then directed Fang, "Explain Spoke's plan to Kaipo. See what he thinks."

Fang explained that he, Kaipo, and Bee would go after the prisoner hut with four other SEALs. Kaipo looked surprised. Fang then said the remainder of his men would go with Spoke and attack with the Expo Team away from the huts. He then asked which direction was the main group of huts.

Kaipo looked startled. "All around in jungle."

Squatting down, he drew in the dirt. Highlighted by a small, red flashlight, Kaipo drew an oblong circle.

"Huts over here. Drug factory here. Prisoners here. Road here."

So far, everything looked fairly close to the original pictures and drawings except for the concentration of huts, the village. The location of the new number of huts was indeed a surprise.

It was also obvious that the main reason the extra help had been supplied was to ensure the drug warlord would know he was being replaced by his rival. The real question was just how much help these men would be when it all hit the fan. Was their commitment more to the drugs, their boss or free the captives?

Spoke knew this whole thing was shaky and felt the pressure that must be going through Bee's mind. It was his team. It was his life. Yes, it was the little girls' lives, but they weren't even sure the correct little girls were in that camp.

They all realized none of them would never be able to stop child slaving. They would never stop drugs. So what the hell were they doing here? This was just crazy. All their lives on the line for an unbeatable foe. Humans would always be greedy and always look for ways to destroy their own lives, be it drugs or slavery. The worst problem was that there were always going to be those that would use this fault in the human psyche for profit.

Well, it won't help to wonder what would be or what could be, they were committed. They couldn't change mankind, but they could rob the dark side of this victory. Some families would benefit from their efforts. Some kids would have a life and some amazing stories to tell their children.

Bee motioned the group to gather up. Kaipo and Fang stood together. Bee told the team that everything was basically the same, but the extra men would go with Spoke, Senior Chief and the Expo Team. "Kaipo, tell your men that Spoke will direct them where and when to attack. Tell them not to shoot the good guys or the kids."

Kaipo translated. Fang nodded assurance the translation was correct. Bee noted the nods and turned to Kaipo. "Let's get going." The team saddled up as did Kaipo's men. They still had hours to go before they slept, as the poet said.

CHAPTER 33 – THE PLAN COMES TOGETHER

The team crested the hill overlooking the drug and human trafficking camp. The smoke from smoldering cooking fires gave the area a lightly smoggy appearance.

The partly cloudy day indicated a high-pressure that seemed to foretell the future weather. That could be good or could be bad. Good, in that the rain would not be dripping down their back and putting out fuses on their pyro techniques. Bad, in that every move would have to be extremely careful.

Even though sunshine would make their movements easier to see, it would have the soporific effect on their guards; they would hopefully be a bit more relaxed, even sleepy. Spoke reflected on the bandit that punished his man with two rounds of 7.62x39. Justice was swift in this world and it was terminal. It was the Law of Tooth and Fang.

Kaipo whispered to Bee that this is where both teams should separate to keep the most cover and protection for them.

Bee looked again at the surrounding terrain. He motioned to Kaipo to show how far the huts extended beyond the clearing. Kaipo returned the motions by pointing some ways farther into the jungle than the original pictures showed. Perhaps this was a good thing that Kaipo had the extra manpower along.

Bee knew if Kaipo had asked "permission" first, he would have been vehemently against it. Perhaps in this case "forgiveness" would be the better route.

Bee motioned to Spoke to take his team and leave. Spoke and Senior Chief LaMonde gathered up their three plus the nine supplied by Kaipo. Fourteen men moving in bright sunlight through the jungle was not exactly the easiest thing to do.

Bee, Fang, Kaipo, Obermeyer and Mitchell waited for almost 35 minutes before moving. They were waiting and watching for the Senior Chief's mirror signal which would indicate that they were in position and ready. This would mean all was about to go hot.

Timing would be everything. The Extraction/Fire Team would have to be in position for the beginning of the Expo Team's diversion.

Slowly, quietly the Expo Team moved through the jungle. Senior Chief led followed by Spoke, Alamasanunu, Barker and Lewis saw the hut almost simultaneously. Lewis motioned for the trailing men to stop and remain still.

Senior Chief motioned to Alamasanunu to move forward and scout the hut. For a big man, the Polynesian had stealth all over him. Carefully, he moved forward. He saw a woman standing in the door of the hut. She did not see him. She looked over toward the camp. Turning, she walked back into the hut.

A young child began to cry. The sound carried through the jungle and tore at Spoke's heartstrings. He only prayed that this woman, this mother, would not endanger the child or children in the hut. He also saw no older children. Was that because they surrendered their children to the horrors of child slavery or to working in the drug processing huts? The thought chilled him.

Alamasanunu motioned that there was no one else in the hut besides the woman and her child. The real question was whether she was armed and would respond if threatened by any incursion into the camp. Carefully he moved back to the Senior Chief.

Giving the hut wide birth they moved on through the jungle toward the main trail into the camp. Once there, they watched and waited.

The clouds marched slowly across the sky. As one cloud began to cast its slowly progressing shadow across the camp, Senior Chief motioned to Kaipo's men to move across the road. They were to move farther north about 200 yards. There they were to spread out to form a rough skirmish line.

When the fireworks started, they were to open up from the edge of the jungle and keep firing. They had to make everyone believe, not just think, but really believe, the attack was coming from their position.

The remaining four unpacked and began setting their fireworks display up. Lots of noise. Lots of noise. Heavy duty fireworks with only the best for our friends, thought Spoke. Noise-type mortar shells aimed to explode both up in the air and aimed toward the ground. Lots of noise. No color, just horrific noise. If this wasn't so serious this could almost be fun. Lots of the good, dense-sounding noise bounced back by the jungle canopy and amplified as only Mother Nature could. The thoughts raced through Spoke's head. This had to work.

Bee waited and watched. Mitchell waited in the over-watch position as the other four moved into position. Fang and Kaipo focused on the hut Kaipo had photographed as the holding center for the abducted children. A woman walked away from the hut. Several men with AK-47s moved to both sides of the door. Another walked around the hut to the east side to relieve himself.

A teenaged woman walked in carrying a basket. One of the guards at the door followed her. A muffled scream came from within the hut. A sharp slap silenced the scream.

Bee wanted to go now, but knew the peril he would stand and the danger to his team and the op. Quietly he waited, ready to dispose of these animals. Hell may have no fury like a scorned woman, but hell apparently never saw a really pissed off SEAL.

A few minutes later, the guard hitching up his pants appeared in the hut doorway. He grabbed his AK-47 and ammo pouches and moved again outside the door.

The flash was small, but clearly artificial. There it was again. The sun would clearly be in the eyes of anyone trying to locate and fire against the Expo Team. In half an hour it would be at the horizon. It was time to move or wait another day.

They did have the luxury of an extra day due to their quick march, but Bee knew not to tempt fate. They had the opportunity now. Take advantage of the day in case there were problems on the egress.

Moments dragged on. People began to stir, moving from one hut to another. Women moved from one of the central huts toward huts in the jungle. The smell of wood and charcoal cooking fires began to waft across the open area.

Suddenly whatever occurred moments before was quickly forgotten. The first explosion caught everyone totally flatfooted. Then five more. Then all hell broke loose.

Explosions and gunfire filled the air. Men began running from outlying areas to the camp. The bushes seemed to come alive with noise and bullets. Men dove for cover. The noise was deafening. The trees forced the sound to echo and reverberate back against the ground.

Explosions kept coming in spite of lulls in the gunfire. The ground seemed to shake with the noise. Finally, the startled village men started shooting back. This return fire appeared to come from the cover of the drug processing hut. They obviously didn't know where to shoot, but were aiming in the general direction. This was always the worst kind of firing, since stray bullets were unusually far more dangerous than aimed ones. Who knew who was a good shot or who was just lucky. A lucky hit spelled just as much trouble as an aimed hit.

Bee waited, observing that even the guards at the prisoner hut were distracted toward the noise of the explosions and gunfire.

Bee, Obermeyer, Fang and Kaipo moved toward the hut. Bee and Obermeyer edged toward the door. Each had their knives drawn. Both grabbed the guards with hands over their mouths and pulled them backwards forcing them off balance. They quickly drove their stilettos up through the diaphragm and into the heart. Both guards succumbed rapidly.

Each rescuer moved into the hut. The noise seemed to increase from the jungle and village helping cover the rearward attack. Obermeyer remained just inside the door. Bee, Fang and Kaipo entered the hut. The sight sickened them.

Before them were 27 children, mostly girls, stripped naked and chained to each other laying in disorganized piles of dirty, feces-laced straw with hordes of flies. There were two women in their early twenties standing next to the children. Both started to scream but were cut off by Fang who told them to be quiet and they would live. He told them to free the children.

Each woman moved with keys to comply. As one bent over to free a young blond girl however, the "jailor" turned and with a horribly ugly leer thrust a knife at Bee. Bee grabbed the woman and moving inside her thrust, forced the knife into her stomach. She stiffened up. Bee then finished the job with his own stiletto.

The children, some of whom were obviously drugged, stared without uttering a sound.

The other woman realizing her companion was dead, quickly freed the remaining children. She then stepped aside. She spoke to Kaipo and asked that she too be freed with the children. She explained she once was part of that same nightmare. As a child she'd been forced to repeat the horrors they were going to go through.

Kaipo translated and relayed the message to Bee. Fang nodded that indeed that is what had been said to Kaipo. Bee nodded and had Fang relay that if she so much as blinked wrong, she would end up like her companion.

The entire evolution had taken less than two minutes. Bee moved to the door and made sure Obermeyer confirmed the coast was clear. They had to move about 20 yards to the perimeter foliage.

Each child that could run was encouraged to follow Bee who had grabbed two of the non-ambulatory children, one under each arm. Obermeyer also moved inside the hut and did the same. Fang and Kaipo followed as well as the woman who carried one young girl. Those that could run, ran behind Bee.

Four children remained still on the hut's floor, unable to move. Depositing his two children on the ground at the edge of the jungle, Bee ran back to the hut and grabbed two more. The remaining two began to cry for fear they would be left behind. Suddenly, Fang appeared in the door and grabbed the last two.

Outside, the Expo Team fired the biggest and loudest bombs which they had saved for last. A huge finale screamed into the compound. Huge explosions and whistles from torpedoes sounded everywhere.

All the occupants of the site were laying low wondering what on earth had happened. Several men started to get up and shoot back only to be cut down by aimed rifle fire from the jungle.

A man, obviously a leader of the camp, tried to rally his men and took four bullets for his trouble. Three other men likewise wanted to be heroes only to join their leader. The rest began to move to the north and into the jungle, firing blindly at the overwhelmingly great force that had arrayed itself against them.

Then, as quickly as it started, the sound ceased. It had all happened in under five minutes. Five minutes that would put the fear of God in every one of them. Five minutes that had seemed like five hours.

Kaipo's men moved farther back into the jungle. Spoke, the Senior Chief and the remaining SEALS also moved back into the jungle.

Now they had to regroup and head south. Sporadic rifle fire continued from the camp as pinned-down men tried to shoot at shadows which they presumed were their attackers. It was a waste of ammo.

Both the Expo Team and the Extraction/Fire Team had their next goal – reach point X-ray.

Within five minutes, the first of Kaipo's men arrived with the Expo Team SEALS. Another five minutes dragged on until the last of his men straggled in. Two had sustained minor grazing wounds. One had fallen and had a puncture wound from a stick.

Alamasanunu quickly dressed the wounds and the group headed south. Spoke and the Senior Chief knew the children would be a load for the Extraction/Fire Team. They began to circle toward the egress trail they would have to take.

Within 30 minutes, they linked up.

Kaipo's men that were unwounded each took a child. Each of the SEALS took a child as did Spoke and Fang. The woman acted as herdsman for the rest of the group. Now Bee was glad he'd added a day.

The rear guard was taken up by the walking wounded from Kaipo's men. If the men from the camp were able to get organized fast enough, they would start looking for not only the attacking force, but the children as well. Bee didn't need a firefight with all these kids.

2120, Five miles from the drug village

Their progress was slow especially in the dark. Frequent stops for small legs and those whose drugs had started to really wear off became a necessity.

It broke each of the men's hearts to see some of the children starting into deeper withdrawal pains. Their crying had to be addressed, but they also had to keep moving away from the camp.

The stop and start travel was excruciatingly slow. Bee realized that he was thankful the bad guys didn't have air support.

Lewis got on his radio and began requesting the extraction be earlier than planned. The response was negative. Assets would not be available for either CAP or extraction until at least Wednesday late afternoon. Bee had to adjust his timing to match the existing plan.

Just great, thought Bee. Here we are with all these children, some wounded, all in withdrawal pain, and we have to spend over an extra day possibly under fire just to wait for our ride out.

Fortunately, the march was slow at best. It would take the extra day just to get to the extraction point.

At daybreak, Bee would stop and make a sort of camp. The problem was whether or not the bad guys could get organized without their leaders to mount a counter attack. Bee knew fires were out of the question, but maybe the cold food they'd brought might help calm and quiet the children.

Several of the previously ambulatory ones were already needing to be carried. He allowed his mind to think of Sandy. What would she do to help these children? He really missed her. He would have to remedy that if she was willing.

Bee's mind was quickly startled back to reality when one of the children screamed as she woke up from a very horrifying dream. The horrible dreams coupled with the drug withdrawal were already starting to manifest themselves.

The young woman who'd also accompanied the children, Chunhua, moved quickly to the child to hold her. This would be their constant concern and frustration for the next couple of days.

Better get used to it, Bee mused. The short 10-minute rest stop concluded. The column moved on. Shoeless children dragging along stepping on twigs and rocks, their feet cut, bruised and badly mutilated. The pain of their situation at least overcome by the remaining effects of drugs. Those that were in fuller withdrawal were the ones moaning or crying.

They continued looking like a file of automatons.

0430, Twelve miles from the drug village

Bee called a halt and motioned for Lewis to bring up the radio. Spoke, Senior Chief and Fang faced Kaipo. Quietly, he asked Fang to interpret.

"How far are we from the border?" he asked. Fang interpreted.

Kaipo responded that it was about 12 miles more to the recovery site.

Bee knew if he stopped too soon, the kids would never get started and keep going. He also knew Kaipo's men might figure this was too much and just disappear as well.

He looked at the rest of the very tired men in the small circle. Their eyes were hollow and the lack of sleep and over exertion was very evident. The adrenalin rush had long ago been replaced by abject exhaustion.

"Alright, we'll go until first light and stop for four hours," Bee directed.

Then he motioned to Lewis and the Senior Chief. "Go ahead about 100 yards and call Foxfire with our intentions. If they can accelerate our pick-up, let them know we have some very sick and tired children. We'll need several medics."

"Roger, that Skipper. We'll be back in about 20 minutes."

Foxfire was the call sign of their headquarters. These names changed with each operation and making sure the call signs were kept straight was the radioman's responsibility. However, like every job on the team, there were several back-ups. The team leader obviously knew their call sign, but virtually everyone else did also.

They headed down the trail. They also knew the bad guys were going to be listening. Misinformation was needed. Call signs were the key to this plan.

Arriving at a location far enough down the track, Lewis turned the frequency dial to the appropriate frequency which was different from their ingress frequencies – again safety of the mission and the team.

"Foxfire, Foxfire, Foxfire. This is Little Spark. Over." Nothing, but it might take a while for the operator to recognize their call sign.

"Foxfire, Foxfire, Foxfire. This is Little Spark. Over." Waiting another five seconds yielded nothing but static.

Suddenly, the ray of sunshine occurred. "Little Spark, Little Spark, this is Foxfire. Over."

The relief probably showed in their intonation and voice inflections.

"Foxfire, Little Spark. Numerous petals drying out. Need much more rain. Any chance for a shower earlier than not? Over."

"Little Spark, Foxfire. That is a negative, but will relay the need for rain to help the dried out petals. Over."

"Foxfire, Little Spark. Roger that. Out."

Both men stood and looked at each other. They would have more medical assistance on the extracting helo, but it could not get there any sooner than originally planned.

Senior Chief quietly and flatly stated, "Skipper will be unhappy, but we've done more with less in the past."

CHAPTER 34 – FATHER GOOSE

1615, Point X-ray

Bee admitted he felt like Father Goose with his brood.

Virtually all of the children were in heavy withdrawal pains from the heroin that had been forced into their systems. Whimpering and crying was constant and tore the hearts out of even the hardest members of the team.

To their credit, Kaipo's men had continued to remain with the group caring for and carrying the children. Each of those men had been able to sympathize and endure the crying and problems of the children. Most of the kids now could no longer walk far without assistance.

The woman, Chunhua, continued to help but it was obvious she too suffered from withdrawals. Her heroin use was far worse but to her credit, she suffered in silence. Her sunken, dark rimmed eyes said it all.

Since this was a lightning op, packs carried only the barest of essentials. The few articles of clothing that were extra in packs helped cover the naked young girls most of whom were in the developmental stages of young adulthood. Even though they were horribly sick and hurting, they held to a simple modesty that needed to be addressed.

At the appointed time, Lewis again radioed for extraction.

"Foxfire, Foxfire, Foxfire, this is Little Spark. Over."

The response was immediate as though they had been waiting.

"Little Spark, this is Foxfire. CAP airborne, rain enroute to point X-ray. Petals can be restored. Good luck. Foxfire, out."

Rain on the way meant that there would be additional medical personnel on board. CAP referred to the U.S. Air Force jets that would keep the Laotian Air Force F-5's from bothering the extraction.

Less than five minutes later, the rumble of a CH-53 Jolly Green helo filled the air. Bee popped the smoke flare. The helo began to descend.

The children screamed from fear. Each of the adults tried to calm them down assuring them these were good people. Two U.S. F-100 Thunderchiefs also screamed overhead.

As the Jolly Green settled, the rear ramp of the aircraft was lowered and Bee and the men as well as Chunhua shuttled children into the bird. The crew members strapped the children into the helo. Those who were too weak to move were addressed by the five medics and crew members of the helo.

Kaipo and his men stepped away from the CH-53. Bee looked at Kaipo realizing he probably might never see the man again except as a potential enemy. He saluted him as a gesture of thanks.

The rear of the helo closed up and the bird was airborne. The entire evolution took less than two minutes. The roar and whine of the rotors was almost deafening to the occupants. The ride would be less than 15 minutes. Their destination was Chiang Saen where a C-47 was already spinning up its engines. Flying under 500 feet, the helo seemed to be doing 200 miles an hour.

Then another sound filled the chopper. Two F-5s from Vientiane, Laos, screamed ahead of the chopper. Suddenly, as if on cue, the two F-100s also roared by engaging the F-5s. No guns fired or missiles were launched, but the Laotians just wanted to say in their own inimitable way, we know you are here, now get out.

Below, the field at Chiang Saen meant that the bird was in Thailand. As the Jolly Green set down near the evacuation C-47, the SEALS, Spoke, Fang, Chunhua and the five medical personnel as well as three of the four crewmen from the helo shuttled children to the waiting aircraft.

Once inside and seated, the aircraft taxied to the end of the runway and headed out. Hopefully, this would end the horrible nightmare they were going to face in their lives. They had a big enough burden getting over the heroin, but at least they would have some help to do that.

Bee realized that of the 27 children, four could have been Sarah Mahoney. They would have to wait until they reached the safety of the hospital at Nakhon Phanom, Thailand.

CHAPTER 35 – THE AGONY OF DRUGS

Base Hospital, Nakhon Phanom, Thailand

Twenty-seven children and one adult. Where were they to sleep. The orderly and chief nurse shook their heads. This facility was not designed for this type of activity.

First of all, there were no pediatricians. Secondly, trauma of this nature was not in the operational mission of the staff.

Calls had already been made to the CINCPACFLT rep in Saigon. The wheels were in motion to evac the kids and Chunhua as well as the SEALS, Fang and Spoke to Saigon. Before that, however, Fang had to ask Chunhua some very important questions.

Chunhua sat on the bed, shivering, sweating and obviously suffering from advanced heroin withdrawal. She couldn't sleep.

Over a decade of abuse and the horrors of one man after another doing things that were not spoken of outside those small wretched rooms haunted her thoughts. Such thoughts trimmed with the horrors of bad dream after bad nightmare. She thought of nothing but getting more heroin. She'd do just about anything right now to feel relaxed and not have the ache all over. Her head ached. Her body ached and muscles spasmed. Her mind was thinking of nothing but how to relieve the horrible aches and the awful pain. She didn't think of the children. She could not. Their nightmare would be their own. She had her own to think of. Just make the hurt go away.

Fang walked over and pulled a chair closer. "Chunhua, please may I have a moment?"

The silent response and pain-filled faraway look filled her face. She couldn't speak. Her mind was only thinking of one thing. She started to stand, but sat back down shaking almost uncontrollably, the sweat giving her the appearance of having showered in her clothes.

"Chunhua, please look at me!" commanded Fang.

He was never known for his loud voice, but right now required immediate focus.

The screen around her cot was torn back. Spoke came in and looked at Fang.

"Fang, she's withdrawing!"

Then more insistently quiet, "She's not going to be able to answer anything. Look, I want to find Lian-Na too. But this is not the time to interrogate her. We've got to get her help. She'll come back to reality, but this is not the time. Come on, we'll accompany them to Saigon."

Midnight, Nakhon Phanom, Thailand

The brand new Navy C-9 Nightingale taxied over to the terminal. Getting a bird this fast meant some serious horsepower had been used. The forward door opened as the stairs were wheeled up to the aircraft's port side. The rear ramp/stairs in the tail was also lowered.

The deuce-and-a-half pulled up. The children that could walk were led up the stairs, most crying. Holding hands helped keep them together, but the medics on board still were needed to guide them up the stair and into their seats.

The rear stairs were used to resupply much needed water and towels as well as bandages.

The SEALs as well as medics then carried up the remaining twelve children and handed them to the waiting medics.

Chunhua followed with Fang supporting her. She was extremely unsteady and in obvious pain.

Last, Bee and the six SEALs as well as Spoke climbed the stairs. The crew members made their way to the cabin and the stairs were rolled away. The tail ramp/stairs were raised. The ground crew signaled the pilot and he started his taxi.

An hour later, on the final approach, Spoke leaned over to Bee, "Can Fang remain here in Saigon for a while to help with Chunhua?"

The nod came, and Spoke noticed a concerned look at the same time.

"That wasn't our responsibility. We need to identify and interview these kids. We need Fang. I can't have him off doing his own agenda."

"I understand," Spoke knew the resolve implied in Bee's tone.

The aircraft passengers deplaned with those who could walk going first. The whimpering and crying hadn't ceased the entire flight as the children continued to feel the pains of withdrawal. The team assisted the remainder of the children. Chunhua appeared in very obvious pain and followed the last stretcher with Fang continuing to assist her.

0300, US Army Hospital, Saigon

The hospital orderlies moved among the children doing their best to calm them and offer water as needed. The doctor came over to the SEAL Team Commander.

"We will look carefully again, but remember some of these children have been through some serious neglect and trauma."

This new facility was an enlarged version of the 3rd Field Hospital which was being phased out. The hospital was still not completed, but was being used to capacity anyway. They had quickly become associated with drug abuse treatment and their staff was specially trained to address such issues.

"When can we talk with them?" Bee persisted.

He was just as anxious to fulfill his responsibility as he was to get some sleep, a shower and a decent meal.

"As soon as they are a bit more coherent, Commander," the doctor snapped back. "Right now all they want is to stop hurting. The pictures of your girl have the appearance of two of the patients. One is one of the injured girls and the other appears to be one of the others. Just remember, all of these children are missed by their parents too. We're working as fast as their little bodies will let us."

"Look, I'm sorry. I guess I'm a bit tired and pretty frustrated."

Bee was obviously willing to listen, but still wanted the situation to end.

"Any type of timeline?"

The doctor responded with a good bit of understanding.

"The one uninjured girl may be able to talk in a few hours. She appeared to be the least traumatized. She needs some rest. We've been trying to help her. She looks the best of the group. Perhaps in about eight hours. As the prescribing physician, I prescribe you and your men get hot showers and whatever sleep you can until then."

"Roger that, doc. We'll be back in a few hours," Bee felt almost relieved.

"I need to get to the CINCPACFLT Rep ASAP. Got a phone with an outside line?"

"You're too late. He's already on his way."

The doctor smiled at having one leg up on these super-studs. In reality he was extremely impressed and would never cease to be amazed at their dedication and under-stated bravado.

"He'll be here in about twenty minutes. We called him as soon as we knew you'd landed."

Bee realized there were a lot of people in on this operation as well there should be. He didn't care now, just so long as they weren't out to kill him or his team.

"Is there somewhere I can at least make myself less fragrant?"

"How about if I show you, Sailor? Just follow me." The throaty whisper sent a thrill through Bee. His mind, legs and heart were stunned. It was Sandy. Somehow it only seemed right that she be here too sharing his burden.

CHAPTER 36 – LOVE'S BURDEN LIFTED

0200, U.S. Army Hospital, Saigon

CAPT John R. Morgan walked into the hospital ward. As the new CINCPACFLT Rep he had been in direct contact with ADM Donophan less than an hour ago. He had his marching orders or should it be emphasized, direct orders from the man himself. He was sure it echoed the direct, emphatic orders from SECNAV as well.

"Where's Doctor Shehan?" he asked the orderly in a direct manner, not angry, just all business.

"Right over here," came the disembodied reply. "I'm Doctor Shehan, Captain. Please step over here. I'm working with one of your star witnesses."

CAPT Morgan walked over to one of the injured young girls' beds.

Dr. Shehan stood and smiled, "She'll be back with us in a couple of hours. Right now she's seriously dehydrated and sleeping quietly. Please be aware, her body has had some serious trauma. The best thing for her right now is rest."

"Doctor, I couldn't agree more, but I have to identify her. Can you at least remove a couple of her head bandages?"

"There were two girls who matched the general description given to us by MACV. Let me introduce you to the other. She is still sleeping, too, but perhaps you can at least look."

The doctor rose just as Bee walked in.

"Sir, I'm LCDR Randy Rogers, Team Leader of this operation," said Bee to CAPT Morgan.

"We've narrowed down our search to two young ladies. This one here," he said pointing to the sleeping girl, "And one other who was hurt pretty bad. Due to her injuries, we've been waiting until they could talk with us coherently. They've been drugged, however they appear to be "fresh starts" and should be able to speak to us within a few hours."

"Couldn't you at least do a preliminary I.D.?" CAPT Morgan began.

Bee raised his hand. Quietly and measured, he responded, "Sir, things have been more than a little hectic. We rescued 27, not just one."

CAPT Morgan, quietly dressed-down, responded much more quietly, "I'm sorry, things have been crazy here too, but you are right."

The doctor stepped over to the two. "Gentlemen, could you please resume your discussion out in the hall? We are hoping not to wake these children."

"Of course," responded CAPT Morgan. The two moved over to the door and into the hall.

"Why don't you get some sleep. I'll be back at about 0700. That's an order. And please bring LT Marks also."

"Aye, aye, Sir. 0700 it is. We'll be here."

Bee headed over to Sandy's Bachelor Officer Quarters (BOQ) room. He needed a shower, shave and more than that, he needed her.

Meeting her at the hospital sent his senses into overdrive. He'd had thoughts of her almost every hour while he was out there. He felt amazingly calm and invigorated. He wanted just to talk with her, to see her, to smell the heavenly scent she naturally gave off. He knew he'd fallen hard but didn't care. He thought of her so much and had so much to say that he could hardly contain himself.

Knocking, she opened the door. Her short, black kimono almost reached mid-thigh. The silk garment was loosely tied with a sash. The embroidered design was of two dragons facing each other and surrounded by beautiful flowers. Bee's mind was certain it symbolized both of his minds going out of control to take her in his arms.

The evening light and hot sultry air was punctuated with the emotion of the moment. She smelled of jasmine. Her hair was still damp from an obviously quick shower she'd taken. He knew he smelled of four days on the trail, complete with a mustiness that was his natural, honest self. He wanted to get to a shower, but could not bring himself to stop looking at just how incredibly beautiful, sexy and seductive she was.

He reached forward and she willingly went into his arms. She inhaled not the smell of a careworn and tired warrior, but of a love she craved. A sense of urgency in her voice invited him to come in.

He apologized for his road-weary fragrance. He begged her to let him shower. He wanted to feel his own clean skin against her body.

She smiled and quietly asked, "Can I wash your back, Sailor?"

That did it. He almost came unglued. He loved her so much. He smiled and said that if she wanted, she could wash anywhere she felt impressed to wash.

She giggled seductively. "Anything else, Sailor Boy?"

It was all he could do to get his sweaty, stinking clothes off. She smiled and helped him with his shirt, pulling it over his head. His pants were a different problem altogether. She giggled again.

He struggled to reach the bathroom. Not because she was stopping him, but because he didn't want to leave her. Finally, he exerted all the strength he had and willed the bathroom to come to him. She let his hand trail off and followed him into the small compartment. He quickly turned on the shower. In no time at all, there was hot water.

He stepped into the shower, the wet shower curtain sticking to his muscular, tan body. The water felt really good. He asked her for some shampoo. She teasingly handed it to him around the edge of the shower curtain. Just as he reached for it, she giggled and pulled it away.

"This shower isn't built for two, but in about two seconds you're gonna be in here with me," he tried to sound upset. She openly laughed.

"Come get me, Sailor Boy," she taunted.

"And a bar of soap with a washrag," he tried to command, but his voice just betrayed his desires.

"Alright, Sailor Boy," she giggled again. "Don't be grumpy with me, or I'll give you more than a bar of soap."

"Just you wait," came his reply. The problem was that it stuck in his throat. He wanted her so badly that he couldn't even speak.

Finally, he croaked, "You gonna do my back?"

She walked over to the shower. It was obvious she had dropped pretenses and her kimono as well.

"Sure Sailor Boy," her voice was husky and tense. She reached over to the shower curtain and pulled it aside. That was all it took to seal the deal.

CHAPTER 37 – "JE NE COMPRENDS PAS"

0700, U.S. Army Hospital, Saigon

"Good morning, Commander," Doctor Shehan greeted the SEAL. "Who are your companions?"

"Good morning, doctor. This is LT Kevin Marks and Mr. Hsu. Has CAPT Morgan arrived yet?" Bee looked down the hall toward the Men's Head.

"Good morning, gentlemen," CAPT Morgan walked out of the Men's Head. "LT Marks, I suppose. And you are?" He looked at Fang.

"I am Mr. Hsu," Fang responded. "I am with the team as an interpreter."

"Nice to meet you," CAPT Morgan regarded Fang. "We are obviously working for the same team. I was told about Mr. Hsu by Admiral Donophan, and since you've been vetted by LCDR Rogers, I assume you're alright. Let's get started."

He looked at Spoke,

"LT Marks, ADM Donophan asked me to convey his appreciation for your significant efforts as well."

The group moved into the ward toward the young eight-year-old laying on the bed with a cold compress on her face. The doctor gently touched her and removed the compress.

"You are safe. These men are here to help you. Do you remember your name?" the doctor quietly asked.

"Je ne comprends pas," the young blond looked bewildered and still more than a little scared. She repeated again in French that she didn't understand what they were asking. The team looked at her and at each other. Where was she from?

Spoke switched to French, "What is your name? Where are you from? Where are your parents and family?" She brightened up and the floodgates opened. Spoke raised his hands and started laughing.

"Whoa, whoa. You are speaking too fast."

She sheepishly stopped speaking. She continued in French, but much slower.

"My name is Yvette Suezza. I am from a small town north of Quebec. My family has a cleaning business. When can I go home?"

"Very soon," Spoke smiled and showed her a picture of Sarah Mahoney. "Do you know her?"

She started to reply, but stopped. The eyes said tons. They screamed recognition.

"Do you know her?" Spoke tried again but with more emphasis.

Hesitating slightly, he asked more slowly, "Do you know her?"

Yvette started to cry and replied in French, "She was with us, but was hurt very badly. The men took her away. I have not seen her since."

Spoke turned to the rest of the group. Each of them returned the look. "Thank you," he said. "Did they separate you when she was hurt?"

"No, but she was so badly hurt that no one was allowed to talk to her."

Spoke turned to the doctor.

"Let's look at that other girl."

Turning to Yvette, he said in French, "Thanks, we will get you home as soon as possible to your family."

Quickly the group moved to the other end of the ward. The other girl's bandages were about to be changed.

The nurse stood as the men walked up. The doctor motioned for her to continue removing the bandages. Slowly, the blood encrusted bandages were removed. The nurse carefully applied sterile saline to moisten the gauze. Layer after layer the coverings were removed. There, before the group lay a sweet young lady, badly bruised and still not awake.

The nurse looked up at five smiling men. Before them lay Sarah Mahoney, badly beaten, but still Sarah. CAPT Morgan turned immediately and left.

Bee looked at Fang and Spoke. "Thanks, gentlemen. Not only are we successful, but we've given 26 other families their children back - a world-class gift."

Fang looked on with a look of difficult happiness. He still had questions of Chunhua. There had to be a connection between these traffickers and his own needs. The confusion of being an agent for INTERPOL and a man in love with a beautiful woman whose whole life had been shattered and scarred years ago weighed heavily on his mind.

LCDR Rogers looked with pity at Fang. Turning to Spoke, he asked quietly, "Will he be alright?"

Spoke responded just as quietly, "Aye, Skipper. He just needs a few moments with Chunhua."

"It seems the least we can do to reward him for his efforts," Bee seemed sincerely interested in Fang's plight.

"Doctor, is Chunhua, the older woman, awake yet?" Bee asked.

"She's pretty dehydrated and has had a rough night," he replied. "Perhaps in another few hours. We sedated her to get her to sleep. She's in rough shape."

"I'm going to leave Mr. Hsu here. He needs to ask her a few questions when she comes out of the sedative," replied Bee. "We are going over to the CINCPACFLTREP'S office for our debriefing. We'll be back in an hour or so."

"Why don't you take a little longer, Commander? She will not be out of her sleep for at least 8-10 hours. I realize you men are pretty hyped-up, but you really need some sleep as well – certainly more than you got last night."

The doctor's reply sounded as much like a response as it did like a warning.

"Yes, Sir. Some rack time would be appreciated. You're sure you don't need us back for that amount of time?"

Bee sounded a bit resolved.

"No need. Mr. Hsu can translate what we need. Anything else, I'll contact you through CAPT Morgan."

The doctor sounded like he was now using his rank to emphasize his directive. It sounded a bit like an order to Bee.

"We'll be back around 1700," Bee responded.

He'd need all of the sleep he could get to be back on track with both his team and with Sandy.

191

CHAPTER 38 – ANOTHER LIFE, ANOTHER TIME

1700, U.S. Army Hospital, Saigon

Spoke walked into the hospital ward. A different doctor was standing just inside the room. He nodded to Spoke and motioned toward where Mr. Hsu – Fang – was seated by the bed of Chunhua.

"Has she awakened at all?" asked Spoke.

"She's had some bad dreams, but the sedative is obviously taking the edge off the heroin withdrawal," the doctor confided.

"He is one determined man," he continued.

"He must really be set on getting some answers from her. He hasn't left her side for more than couple of restroom breaks."

"Yes, Sir. He's got a lot at stake here. His wife lost a sister to the human trade business. He's on a quest to find her if possible," responded Spoke.

"What a crime. These innocents have done nothing to merit this kind of horror," the doctor was becoming more animated.

It was obvious he hated the thought of child slavery as well as emphasized with those that had to endure the horrors of loss.

Spoke walked quietly over to Fang. Fang looked up and smiled a wan smile. He was tired.

"Why don't you let me sit here a while, good friend. I'll wake you if you'll permit me to," Spoke quietly stated.

He motioned to the doctor.

"Please show Mr. Hsu a place to lay down."

The doctor motioned for one of the orderlies to escort Mr. Hsu to the other end of the ward where a bed was freshly made up. Fang slowly stood and almost trance-like followed the orderly to the cot. Sitting down, he seemed to fall asleep literally before his head hit the pillow. His boots were carefully removed by the same orderly and he was allowed to lay down.

Spoke kept up the vigil. He mopped the forehead of Chunhua. She slept very poorly and struggled to extract herself from nightmare after nightmare.

As soon as she started to stir, Spoke would lay his hand on her shoulder and pat it gently. Her movement was typical of those extracting themselves from the horror and pain of prolonged drug usage. She obviously didn't want to start this journey down into the depths of hell, but had been forced to do it by some of the world's worst slime on earth.

Spoke reflected on the debrief at the CINCPACFLT rep's office. ADM Donophan was included in the debrief by secure telephone. Spoke had been highly praised for his ingenuity and again knew he had the admiration of those he worked with. This more than likely would never merit a medal or any other recognition, since Intelligence Officers rarely were cited for their actions in the field. That was insignificant since he knew his fellow operatives regarded him in the highest esteem, and that was all that mattered as awards would go. The lives of these young girls would mean that someday, somewhere there would be a family that would now have a mother. Their families would also have them back again and give them the chance to mature without the horror of drugs and prostitution.

Chunhua stirred again and moaned softly. Spoke gently wiped her forehead and face. She opened her eyes almost in a trance. Then she smiled a weak smile and closed them and relaxed.

2300

Chunhua awoke with a start and her eyes reflected the horror of another nightmare. She struggled to sit up. She desperately wanted to get out of there. Her voice, soft, but insistent, wanted to be rid of this vice-like pounding in her head and stomach. She cried. Spoke did his best to keep her tears from flowing on her pillow.

The doctor came over and looked at her chart. This was a different doctor than when Spoke had first come in. He was an Air Force Major and seemed just as concerned as all the staff had been.

"Has her IV been changed?" he asked.

Spoke shook his head negatively.

The doctor motioned for one of the nurses and an orderly to come over.

"It looks like her vein has collapsed. We need to start another IV and get her hydrated."

Both the nurse and the orderly moved to their respective spots as if on cue. One grabbed another IV set-up and the other retrieved a bottle of dextrose water from the nearby cabinet. This was to give her both a limited amount of nourishment in the form of sugar as well as normal saline water to hydrate her.

Looking at her feet, it was very obvious where she had been injecting her heroin. The bruises and sores on her feet and between her toes was disgusting. Men who would use her just for her body didn't care. They didn't look at her feet. They only looked to satisfy their own lusts.

Spoke felt the anger welling up in himself. He had already moved from her side.

He quietly walked down to check on Fang. He was still sleeping. Since he trusted Spoke explicitly, he could relax and find the deep sleep his body required.

The nurse and orderly moved back from the bed. Both looked at him and the nurse subtly motioned with her head that he could come back to his chair. Quietly he went back to sit by her.

Several of the young girls also required attention. They groaned or cried softly. It was quiet and they almost seemed apologetic that they broke the silence.

Fifteen minutes after the change of the IV, Chunhua started to stir with more pronounced determination. She opened her eyes, eyes filled with tears and fear. She tried to talk, but words could not form well. Her voice did, however, carry enough to wake Fang. He jumped up and quickly came down to her bed. He looked at Spoke as if to say, why didn't you wake me?

Spoke just quietly wiped Chunhua's face and talked soothingly to her as if she were a sick child and he were the loving parent that had waited all night for her fever to subside.

Spoke turned to Fang and said, "She just barely came to. I would have had the nurse wake you. She has not said anything that makes any sense."

Fang relaxed and realized he had perhaps been too hasty to think his close friend would let him down.

Spoke motioned that perhaps he could go down and get something from the mess hall. The Army, like the Navy, had a 24/7 mess hall that catered to the medical staff. Since they were awake all hours of the day and night, they needed food as well. The Navy had "mid-rats" which stood for the mid-watch rations. The Army just kept the pot on and the soup and coffee hot.

Spoke said that he would also like something and if Fang would go get something to eat, he could return and spell him long enough for him to get some chow. Fang thought about it for a few seconds and agreed.

"What's good?" he chuckled. "I know, just look at what is on someone's plate and ask for some of that."

Spoke reminded himself that Fang did get some sleep. He was showing his humorous side.

0500, U.S. Army Hospital, Saigon

Fang continued his vigil and Spoke was able to get some sleep for a few hours. Then shortly after 0500, a soft muted moan and several words in Thai indicated a restlessness from the sweat-drenched form of Chunhua. Fang gently touched her shoulder and she opened her tear-filled eyes. She recognized the kind man who had helped her and the others escape. She desperately wanted a fix, but Fang's gentle words denied her that desire.

The soft voices startled Spoke from his sleep and he looked down the room at Fang leaning over Chunhua. He shook off the sleep-deprived cloud in his mind and sat upright. Then getting his bearings, he headed down the ward to stand by Fang.

"She wants more drugs," Fang quietly said. Then a bit more forcefully, "Doctor?"

The doctor came over and looked down at an obviously strung-out patient. Fang continued to comfort her. He quietly shook his head no. She was coming out of her lethargy and needed to feel a bit of pain in order to help her to realize she was part of the real world. He knew she would spend the next several weeks much the same way before coming out of this state.

Fang looked into her eyes and quietly, but earnestly asked if she remembered when she was taken away by the bad men.

She looked confused at first but then a glimmer came into those pain-wrenched eyes and said it was 1961. She was 9 years old. Now she looked like she was over 40 even though she was less than 21.

Again Fang patiently and quietly asked, "Do you remember where you came from?"

She struggled with the formation of the words, but then a spark of reality came back into her eyes.

"Hong Kong," she said quietly.

Fang could hardly contain himself. Slowly and carefully he asked, "Do you remember another girl from Hong Kong named Lian-Na?"

Chunhua again looked blankly at him.

Struggling through the fog and pain, she quietly said, "Yes. We were together for many months."

Fang then patiently continued, "Do you know where she is now or what happened to her?"

"She was taken to Bangkok and sold," the reply was quiet and steady, but obviously filled with emotion.

EPILOGUE – CAN THERE BE A FUTURE?

Fang sat in the gathering darkness of his hotel room. What could he do? How was he supposed to tell the one love of his life the news he'd discovered?

He was due to be back in Kaoshung, Taiwan, in two days. It was his concern for the delicate condition he'd left his love in. Would she be able to understand or accept the answer he found? Mei-Li seemed to be sustained by the hope that she would find her little sister, Lian-Na. He knew she already steeled her emotions to weather even the horrible physical beating she'd taken in Hong Kong. The real test of love would be her ability to take this emotional beating.

Now, with the details from his interview with Chunhua, their meeting a chance so remote that he could not even fathom the infinitesimal, slight possibility it had led to anything. He had to reveal those findings, didn't he? Would he be strong enough to help and assist her in this immense trial?

Waiting in the dark, he needed to figure how to do this so as not to cause his new bride a fatal emotional blow.

The telephone in his room rang.

He picked it up.

"Yes," was all he could say.

"Fang, this is Kevin. Do you have a few minutes?"

"Yes, of course." He tried to sound up-beat and warm to his close friend. "I'll be right up."

A few minutes later the soft knock at the door verified that Kevin had arrived and was waiting. He quietly walked to the door.

"A few of us are downstairs. They wanted to say 'Good bye' to you."

Kevin noticed Fang was remarkably quiet and noticeably upset. He also noted the closed blinds and the lights off. While an excellent reader of human signs, it wouldn't take a genius to see through Fang's façade.

"Did I come at a bad time?"

"No, I was just in thought. Yes, I would like to come down. Let me get myself together."

Fang realized that he'd unconsciously been shedding tears over his dilemma. He needed to wash his face and put on his outward cover. It would not look right to see these strong men with a look of his real human side. Kevin immediately noted his friend's demeanor.

"If you would rather wait for another time, I can let them know."

"No, I want to see them and thank them. I have much to thank them for. Please wait here for me."

Slipping into the bathroom, he splashed some water on his face and chose to change his shirt. Finally, ready, he motioned for Kevin to walk with him.

Arriving in the lobby, he saw the other men of the team. Each greeted him and pressed a sincere and hearty thanks for his help in making it a successful operation.

LCDR Rogers looked deep into Fang's eyes. Fang quickly looked down. Randy then looked over at Kevin as if to say, what's going on? Kevin returned the look with an almost imperceptible shrug of his shoulders.

Again keeping the spirit light, they all invited both Kevin and Fang into the bar for some refreshment. Randy knew Kevin would only have a ginger ale, but he didn't know if the strain on Fang would be enough to cause him to attempt to mask or even drown his feelings with alcohol.

Fang thanked the group and followed them into the bar. He, like Kevin, ordered a ginger ale. Each man thought this was the last they would see of each other, and in that case, wanted to drink to each other's health. Fang rose to the emotional challenge and mixed well for about 20 minutes.

Finally rising, Fang said he needed to finish packing and while grateful, would have to excuse himself. Kevin also said he'd walk out with Fang.

Once on the elevator, Kevin looked at his close friend.

"With the information I now have, I can look much deeper into the time and location Lian-Na was last seen. I will use other resources I have access to. I will keep in touch and let you know when I find something." There was no loss of emotion in the translation of feelings.

Fang felt an equally strong, emotional response. If anyone would and could, Kevin would be that man. He knew of his strong, tender feelings for Mei-Li. He also knew she felt for him as a big sister to her younger brother.

"Thank you, my good friend."